The Inside Scouts
Help the Brave Giraffe

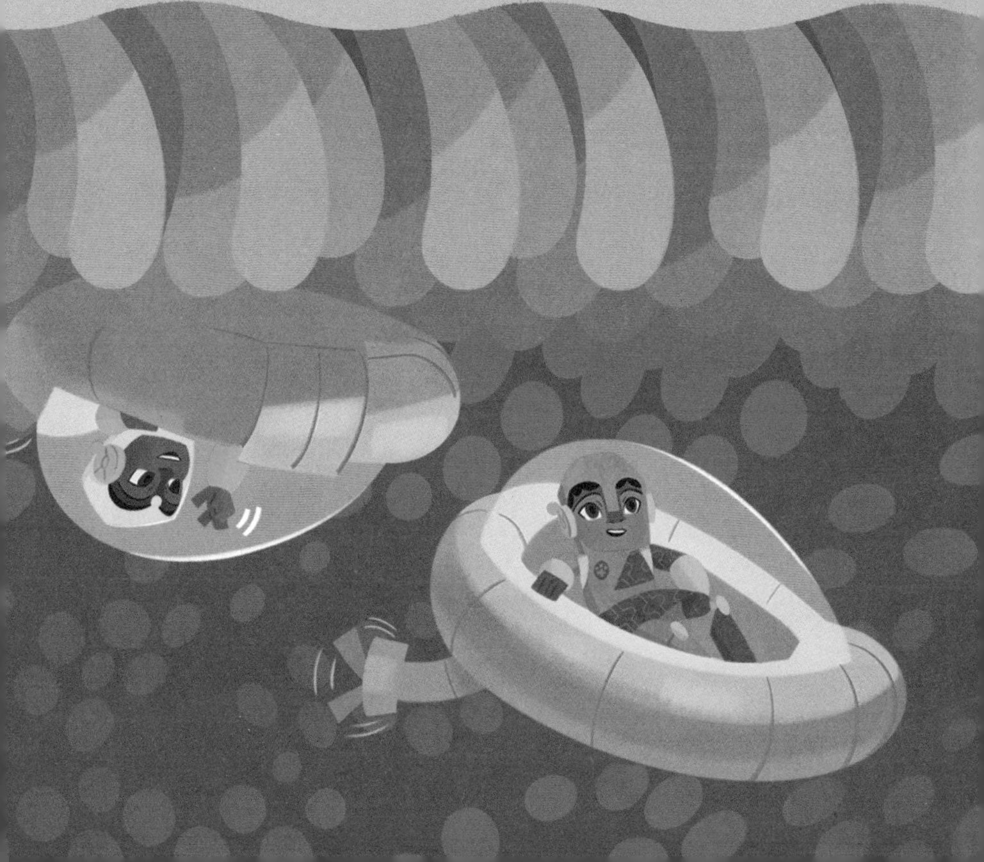

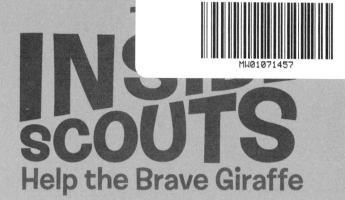

Read more adventures!

THE
INSIDE
SCOUTS
Help the Kind Lion
ACORN
ADVENTURES INSIDE THE BODY!
Written by
Mitali Banerjee Ruths
Art by
Francesca Mahaney
SCHOLASTIC

THE
INSIDE
SCOUTS
Help the Strong Cheetah
ACORN
ADVENTURES INSIDE THE BODY!
Written by
Mitali Banerjee Ruths
Art by
Francesca Mahaney
SCHOLASTIC

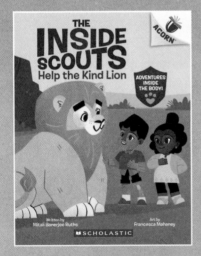

THE INSIDE SCOUTS

Help the Brave Giraffe

Written by
Mitali Banerjee Ruths

Art by
Francesca Mahaney

SCHOLASTIC INC.

With heartfelt thanks to the Rice/Baylor Medical Scholars Program —MBR

To my art teachers and mentors, thank you for all that you do —FM

**Thank you to Christopher Damman, MD,
for sharing his expertise on gastroenterology for this book.**

Text copyright © 2024 by Mitali Banerjee Ruths
Illustrations copyright © 2024 by Francesca Mahaney

Library of Congress Cataloging-in-Publication Data

Names: Ruths, Mitali Banerjee, author. | Mahaney, Francesca, illustrator.
Title: Help the brave giraffe / written by Mitali Banerjee Ruths ;
illustrated by Francesca Mahaney.
Description: First edition. | New York : Scholastic Inc., 2024. | Series:
The inside scouts ; 2 | Audience: Ages 5–7. | Audience: Grades K–2. |
Summary: When a giraffe has tummy trouble, the Inside Scouts must go
down a very long slide into the gut to find out what is stuck in the
stomach. Includes fun facts about the gut.
Identifiers: LCCN 2023009652 (print) |
ISBN 9781338895018 (paperback) | ISBN 9781338895025 (library binding)
Subjects: CYAC: Giraffe—Fiction. | Stomach—Fiction. | Anatomy—Fiction. |
Ability—Fiction. | LCGFT: Picture books.
Classification: LCC PZ7.1.R9 He 2024 (print) | DDC [E]—dc3
LC record available at https://lccn.loc.gov/2023009652

10 9 8 7 6 5 4 3 2 1   24 25 26 27 28
Printed in India   197

First edition, June 2024
Edited by Katie Carella
Book design by Maria Mercado

Table of Contents

Meet the Inside Scouts

They have the power to shrink super small.
They go inside animals to help them feel better.

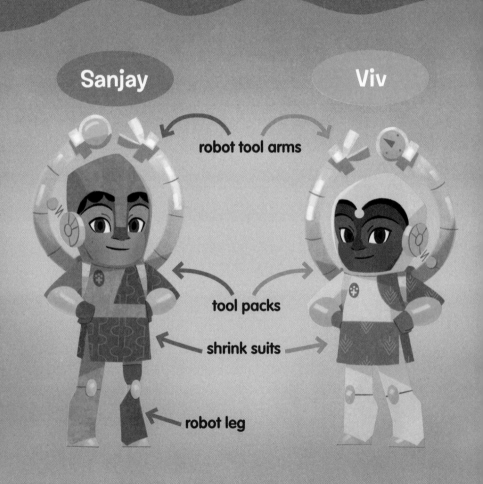

Sanjay

Viv

robot tool arms

tool packs

shrink suits

robot leg

What Is Stuck?

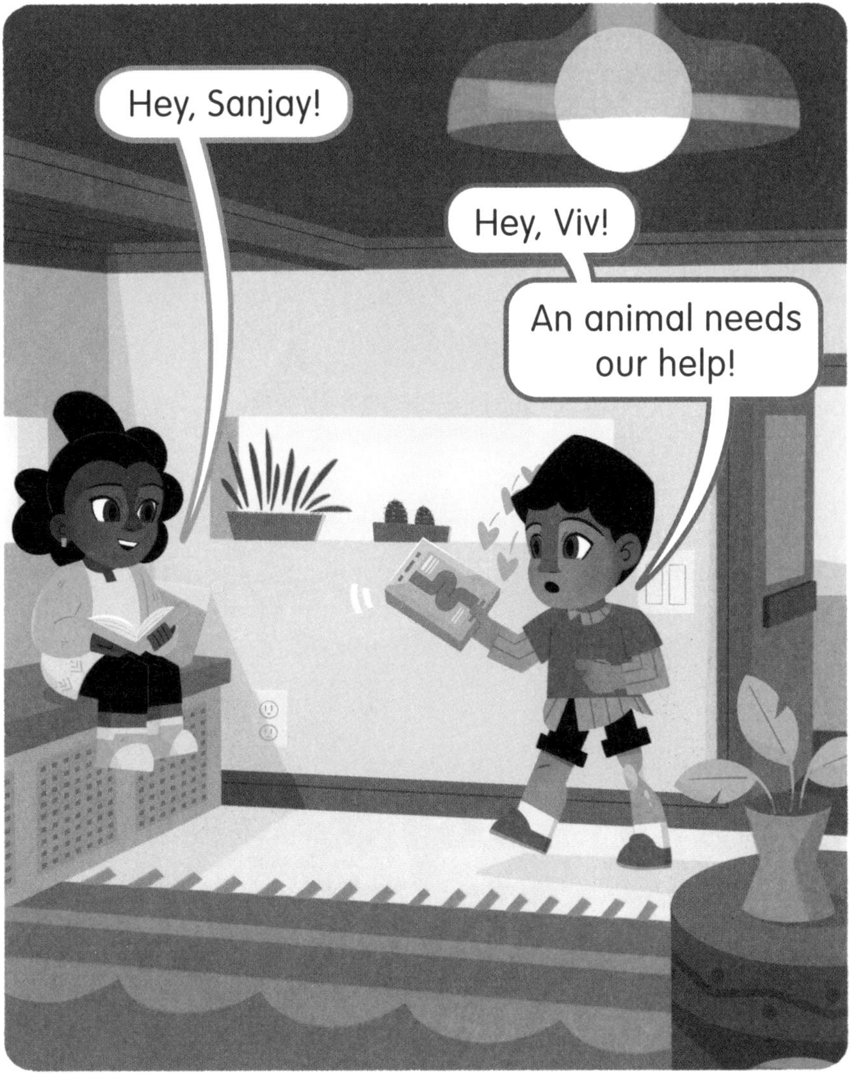
Hey, Sanjay!
Hey, Viv!
An animal needs our help!

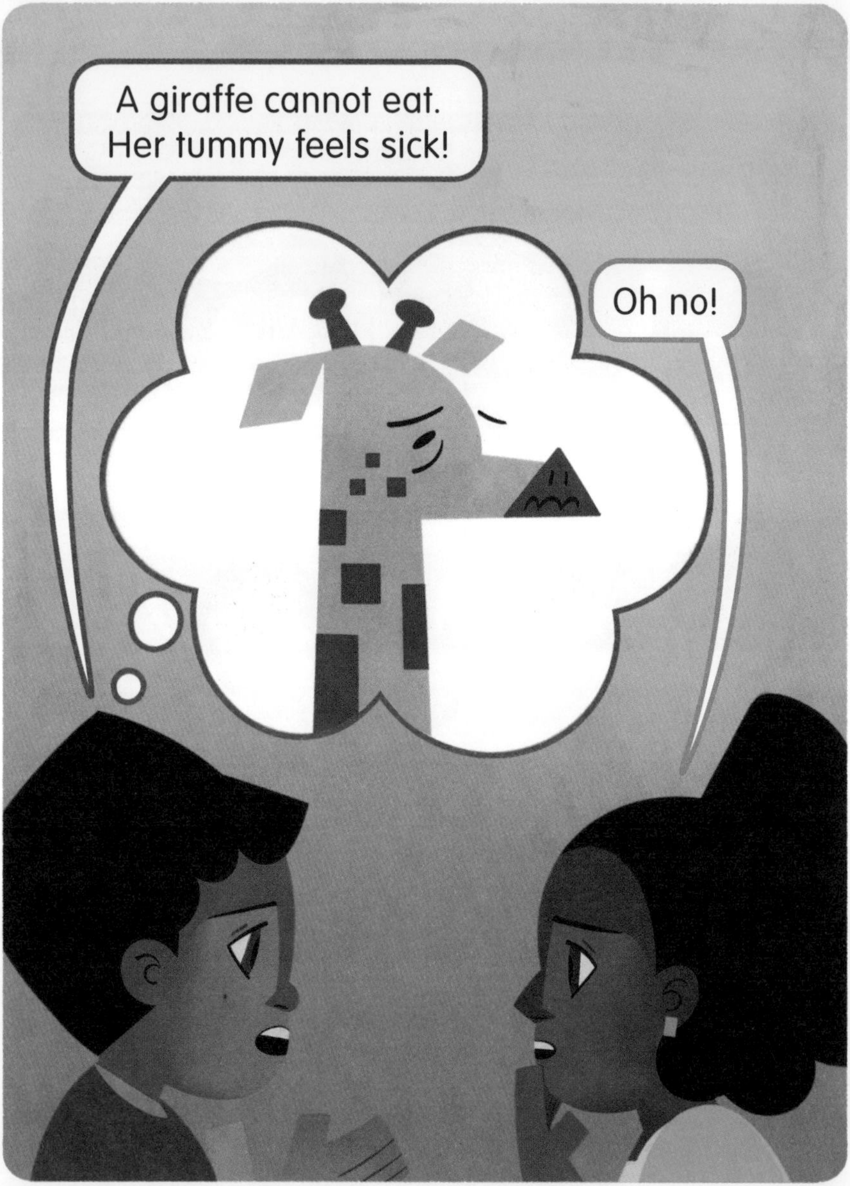
A giraffe cannot eat.
Her tummy feels sick!
Oh no!

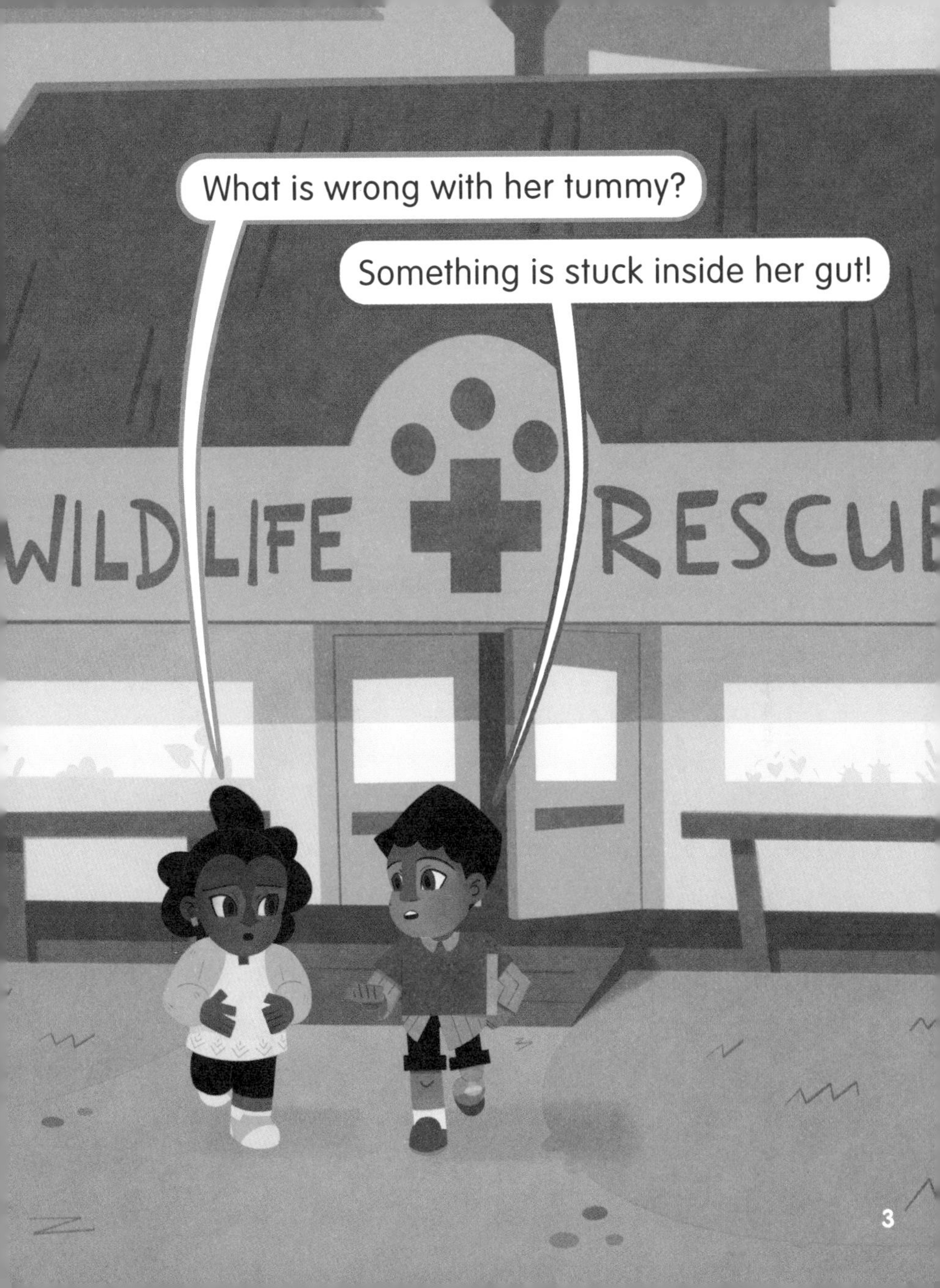
What is wrong with her tummy?
Something is stuck inside her gut!
WILDLIFE RESCUE

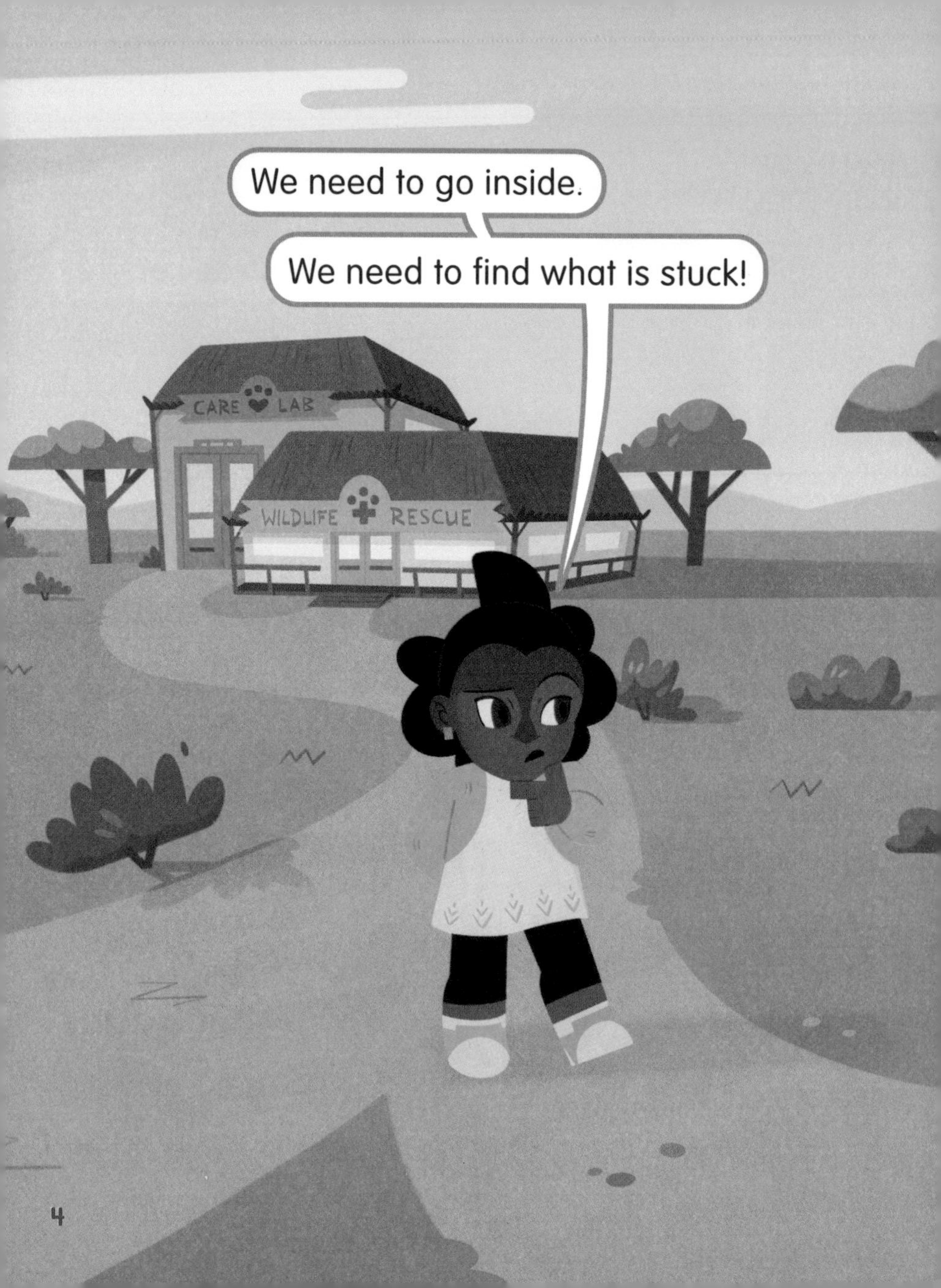
We need to go inside.
We need to find what is stuck!
CARE LAB
WILDLIFE RESCUE

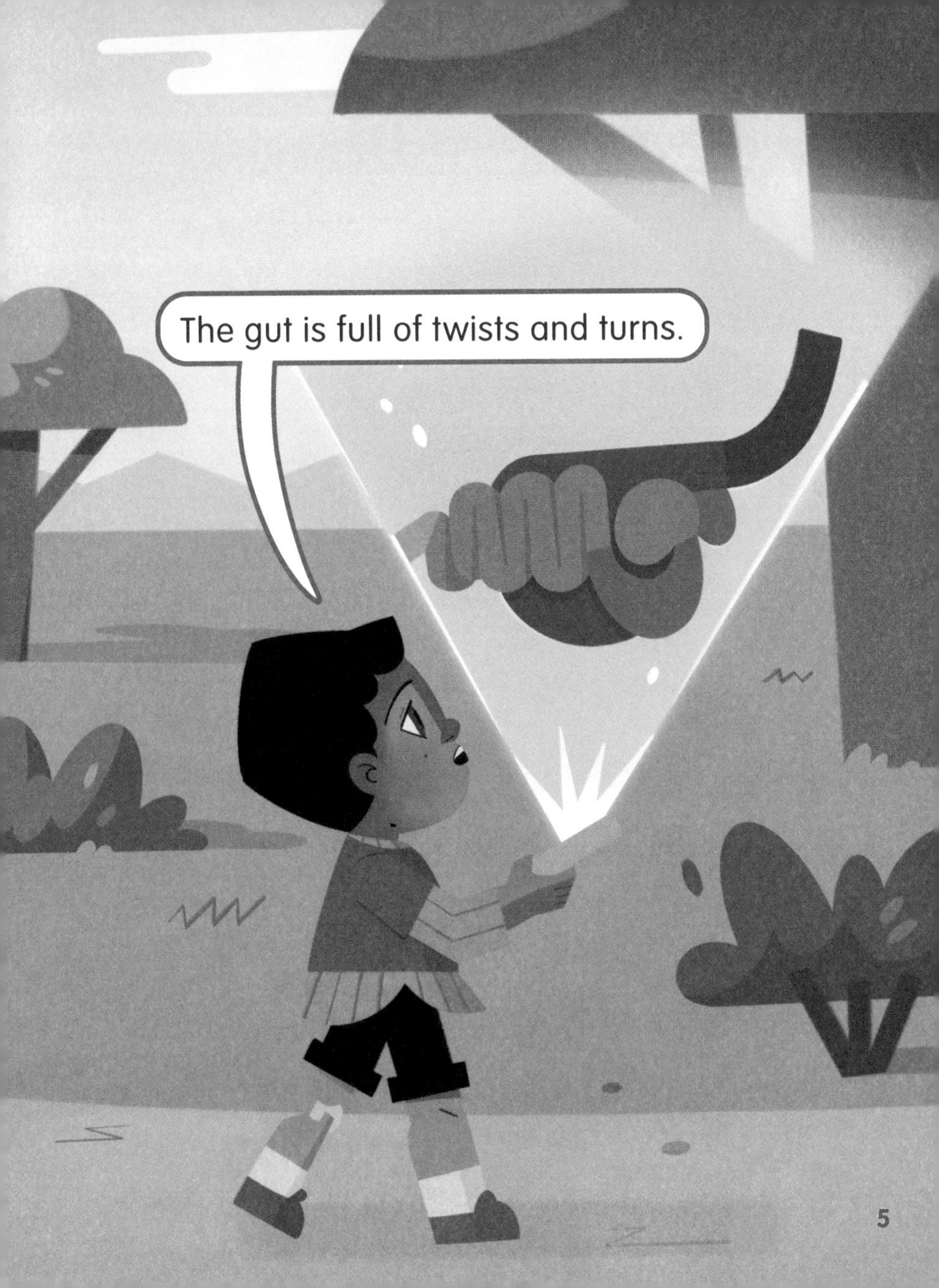
The gut is full of twists and turns.

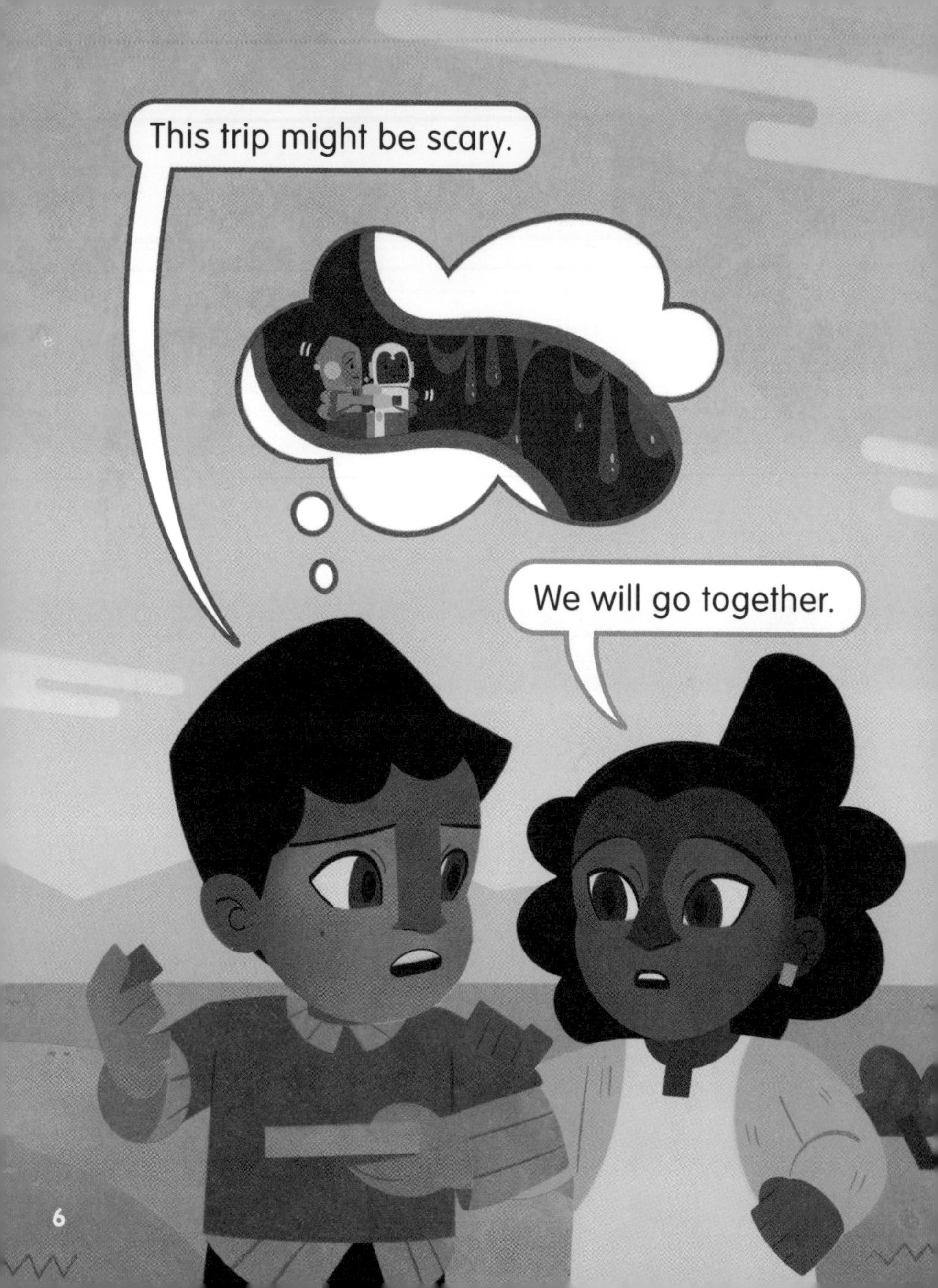
This trip might be scary.
We will go together.

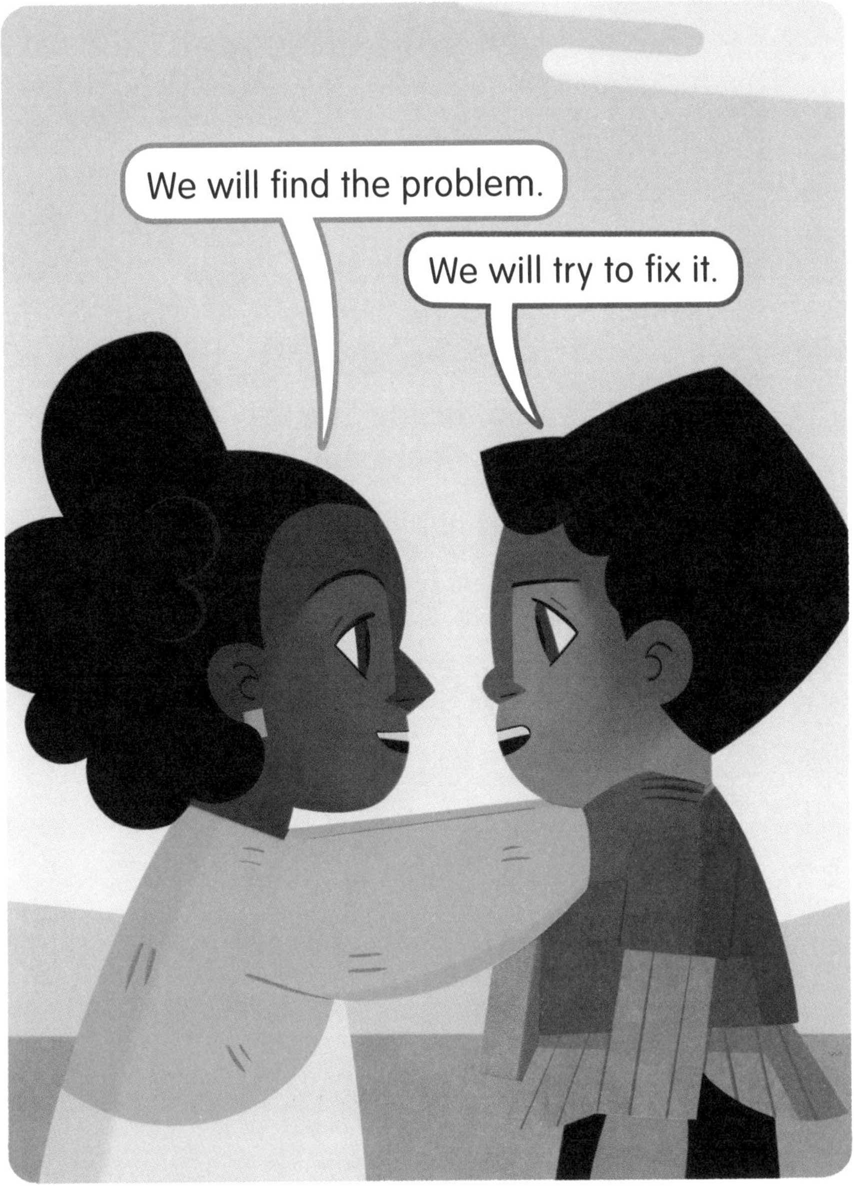
We will find the problem.
We will try to fix it.

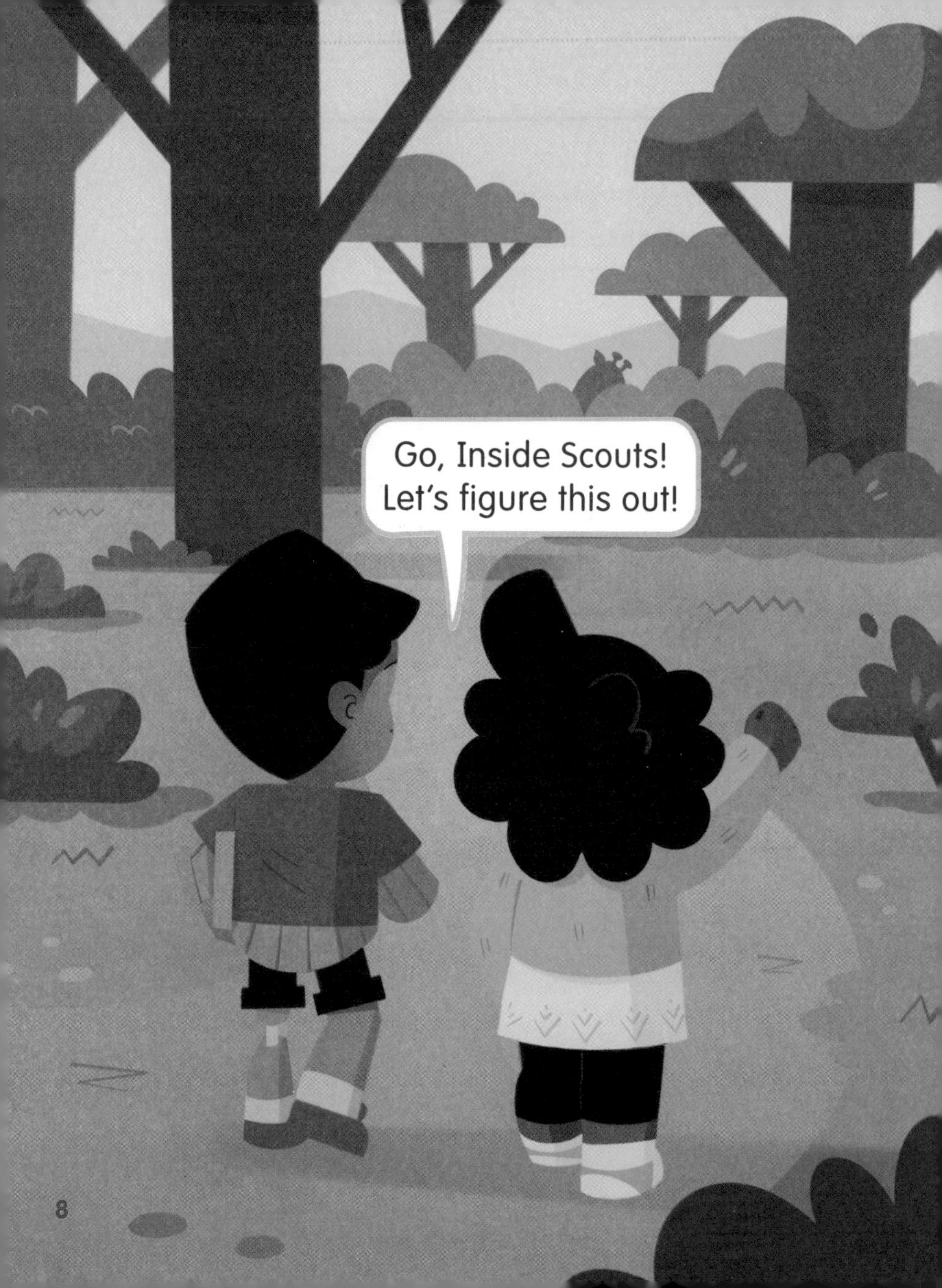
Go, Inside Scouts!
Let's figure this out!

My Tummy Hurts

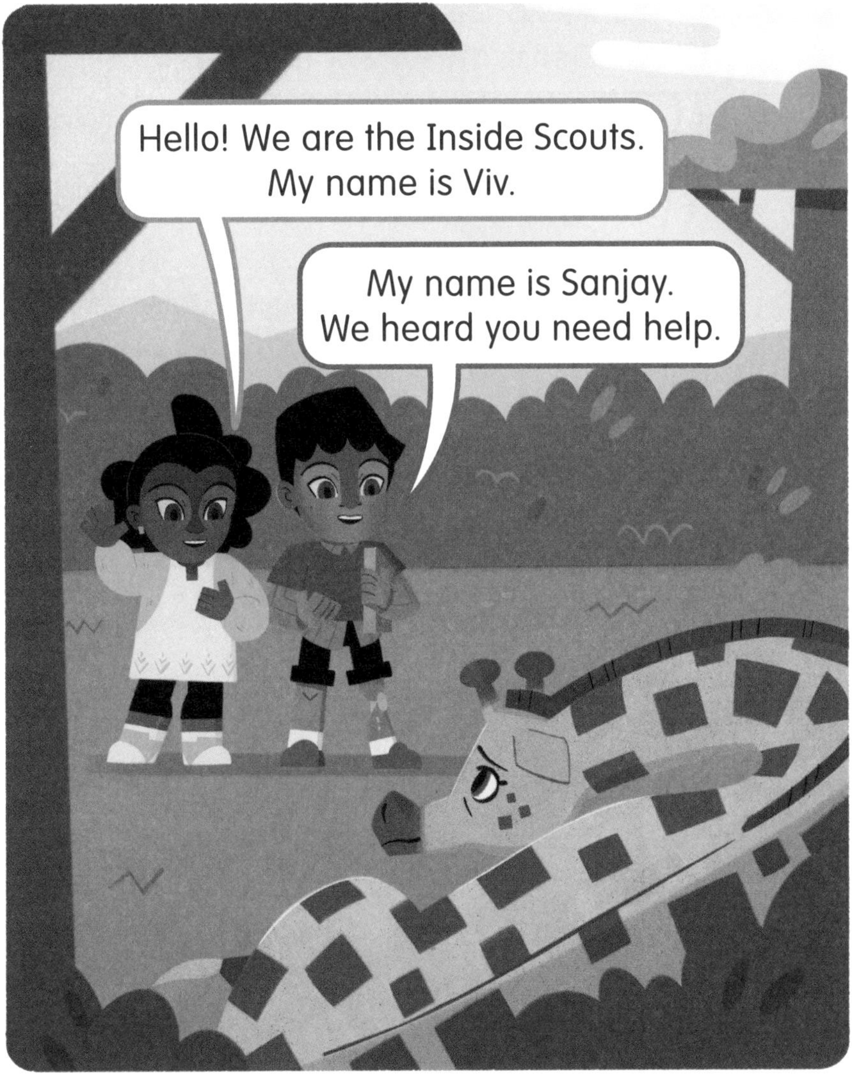
Hello! We are the Inside Scouts. My name is Viv.
My name is Sanjay. We heard you need help.

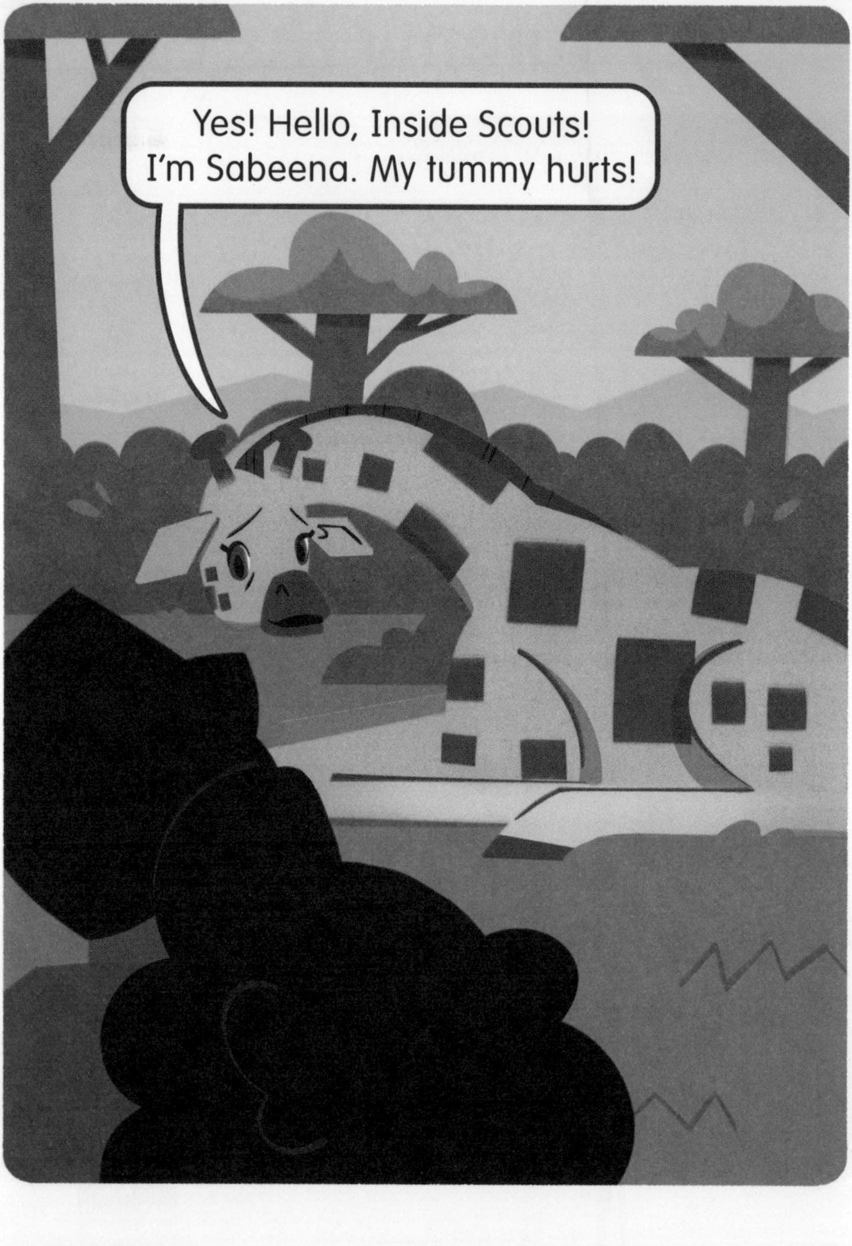
Yes! Hello, Inside Scouts!
I'm Sabeena. My tummy hurts!

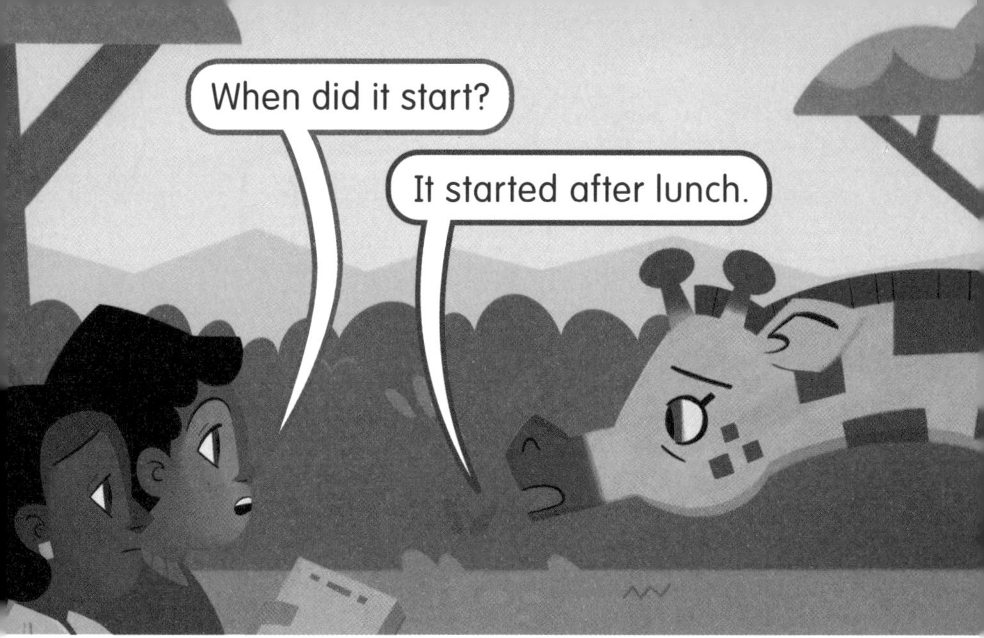
When did it start?
It started after lunch.

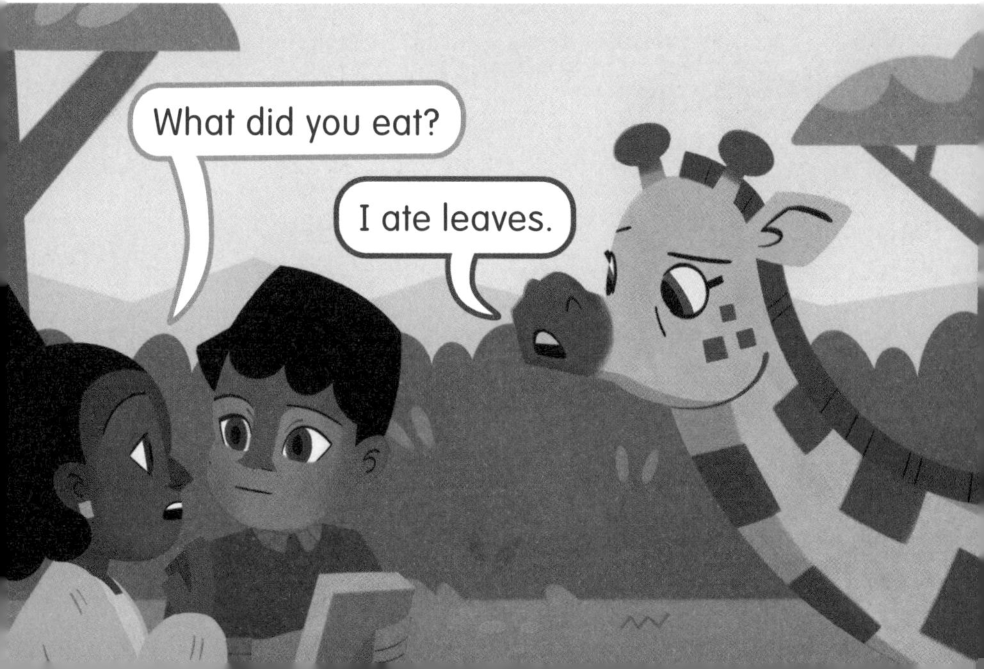
What did you eat?
I ate leaves.

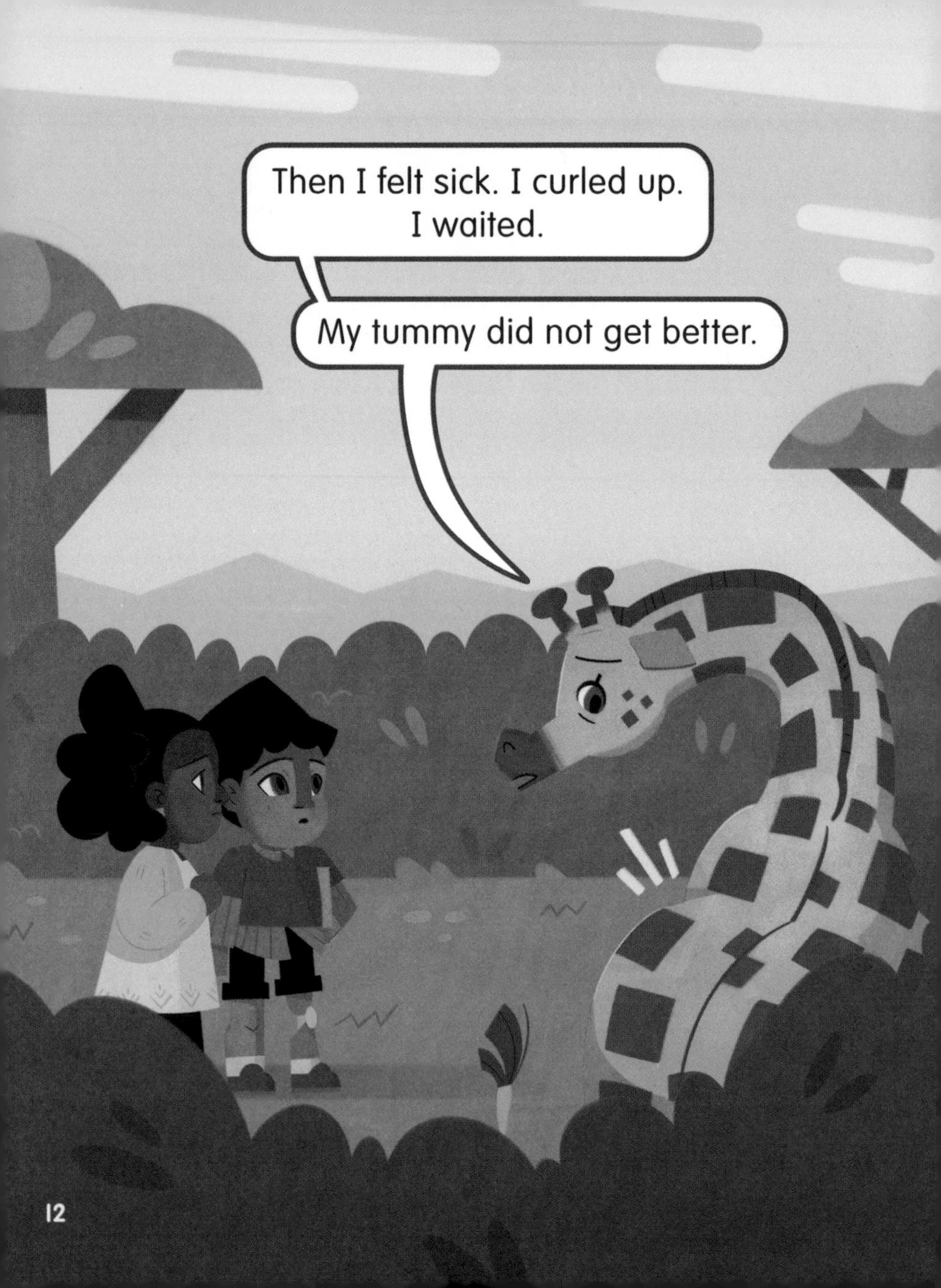
Then I felt sick. I curled up. I waited.
My tummy did not get better.

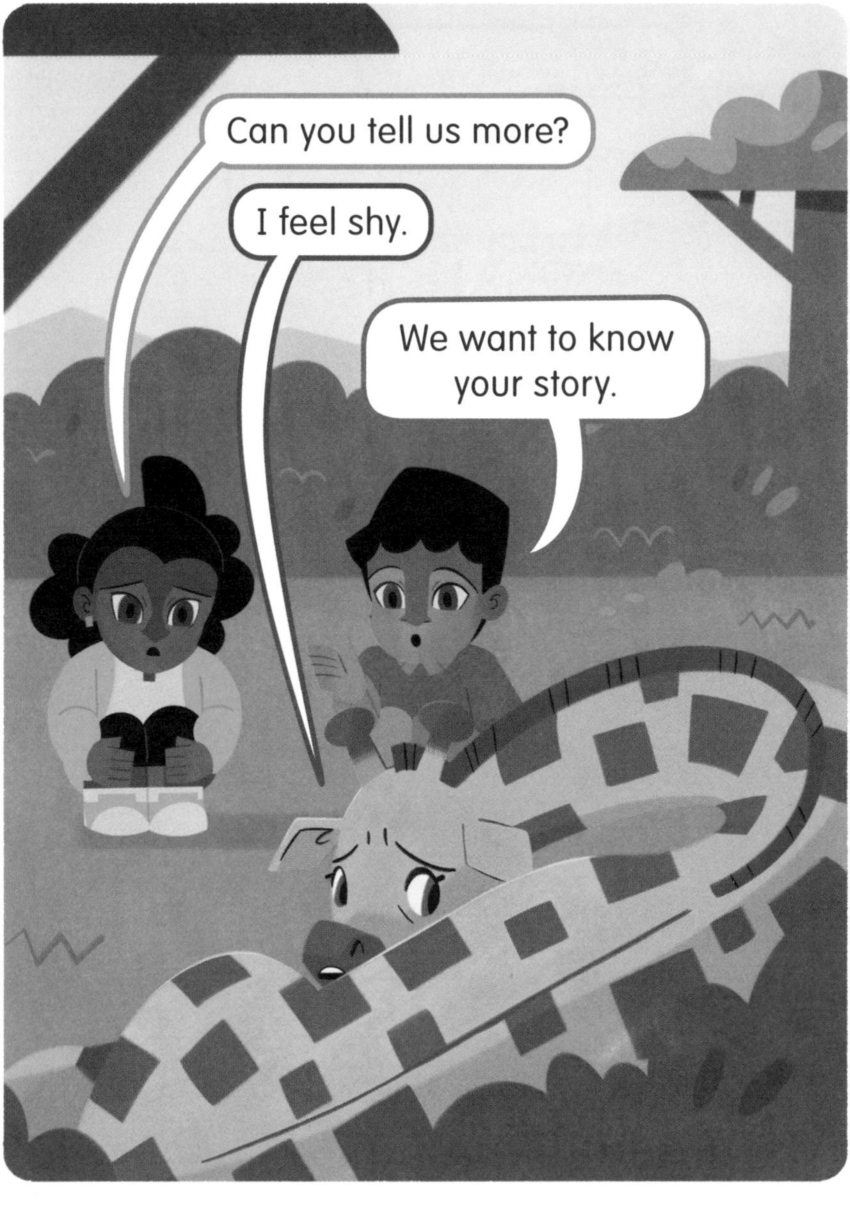
Can you tell us more?
I feel shy.
We want to know your story.

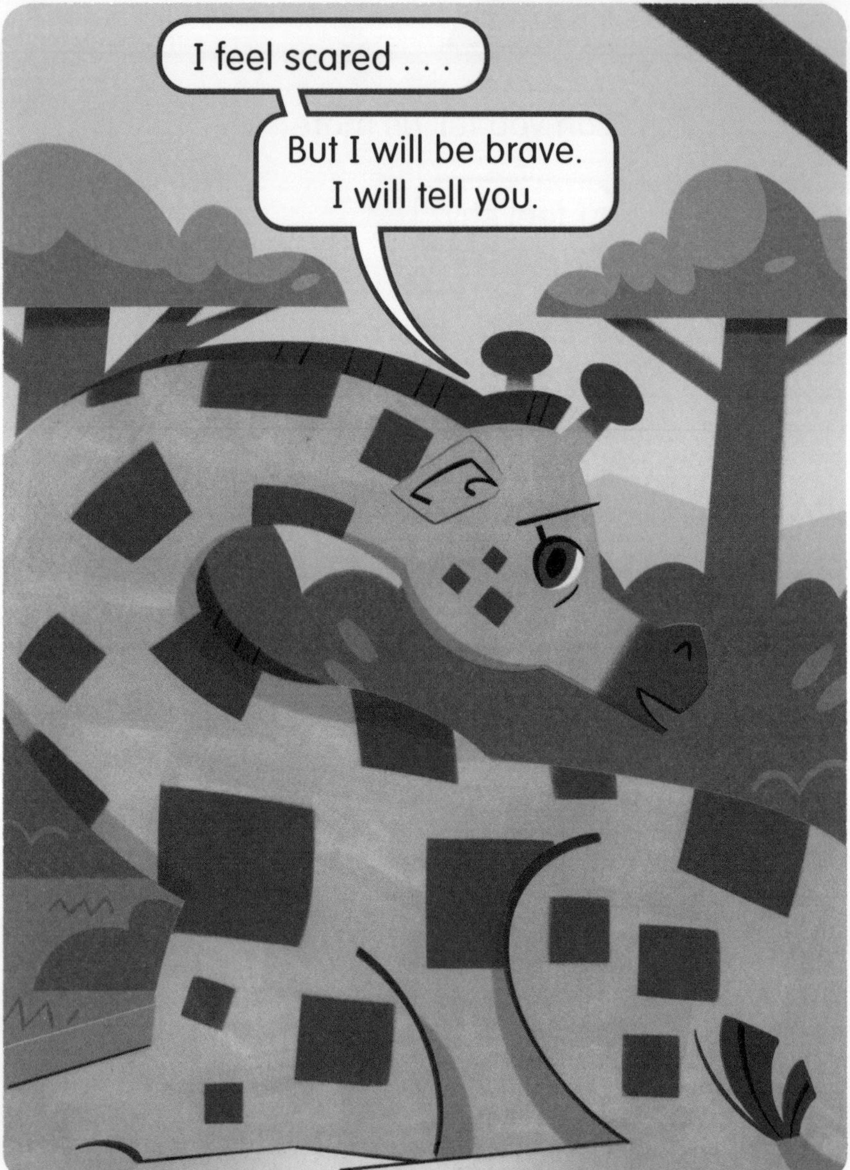
I feel scared . . .
But I will be brave.
I will tell you.

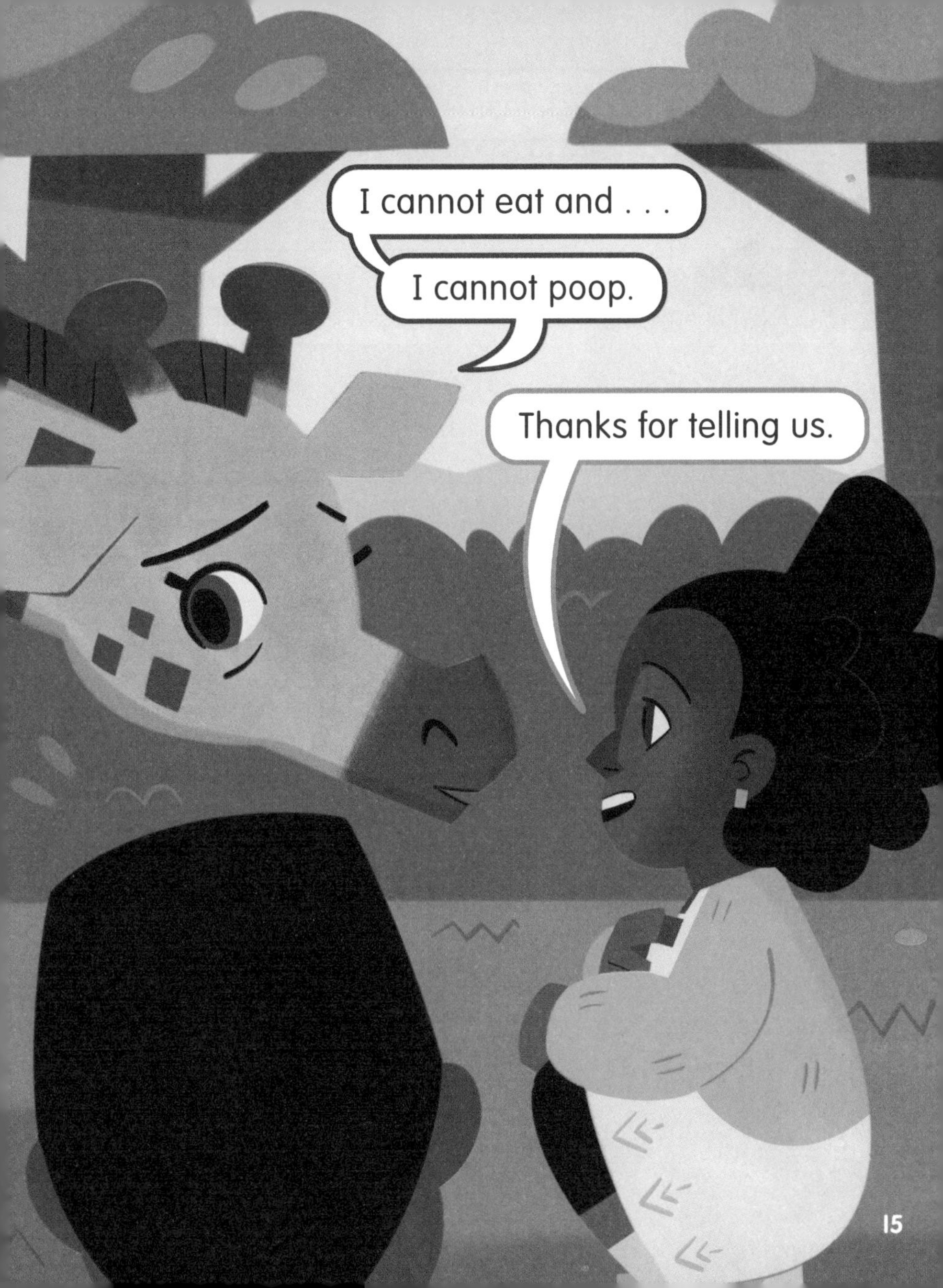
I cannot eat and . . .
I cannot poop.
Thanks for telling us.

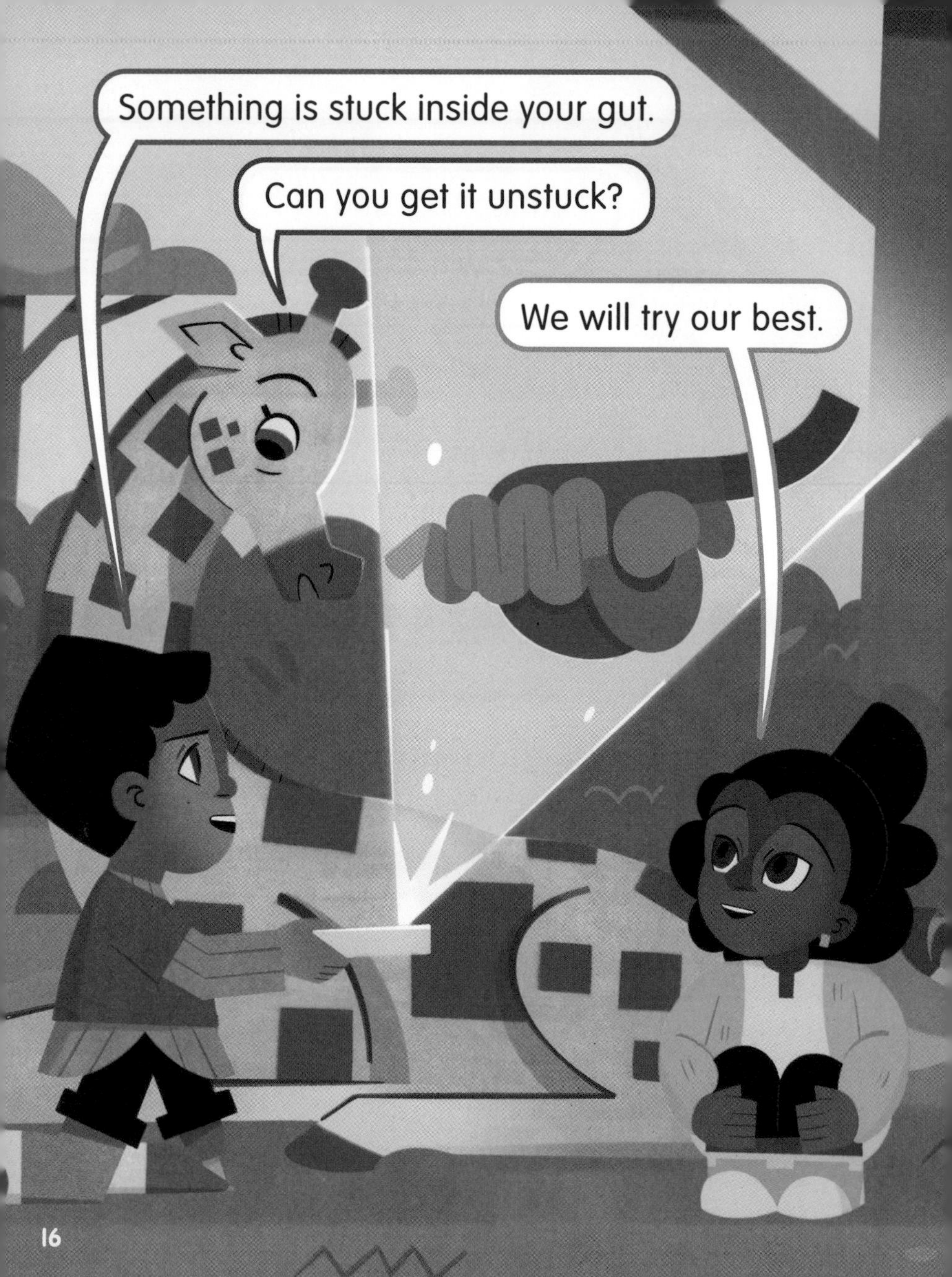
Something is stuck inside your gut.
Can you get it unstuck?
We will try our best.

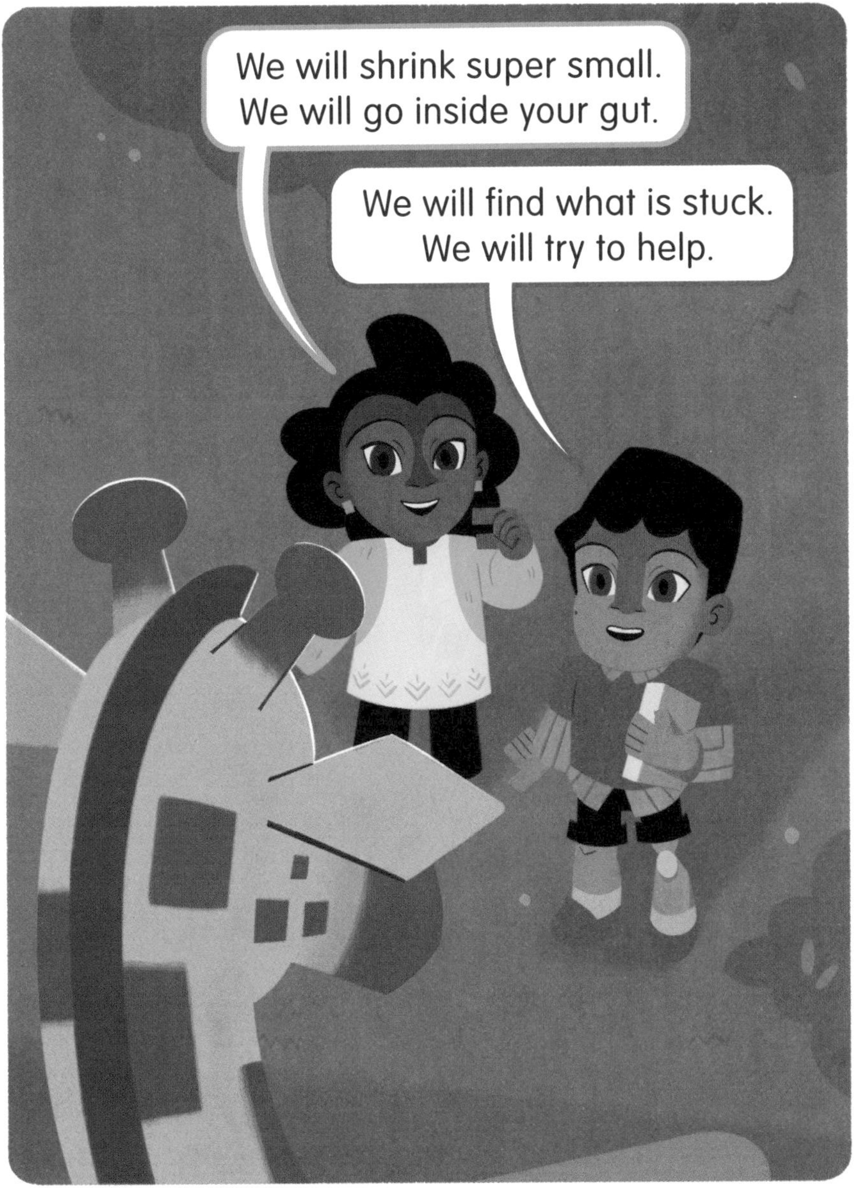
We will shrink super small. We will go inside your gut.
We will find what is stuck. We will try to help.

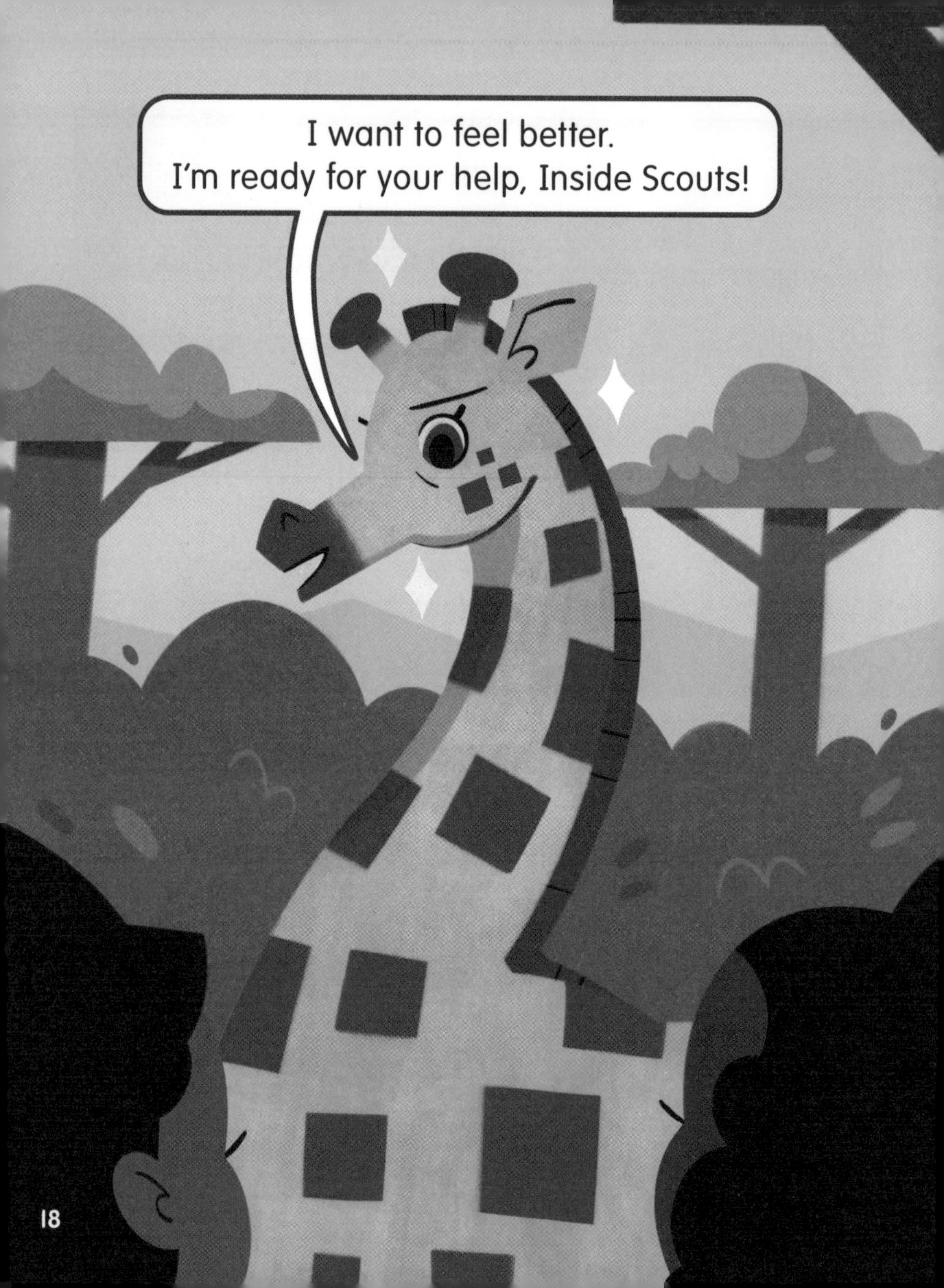
I want to feel better.
I'm ready for your help, Inside Scouts!

Time to Jump!

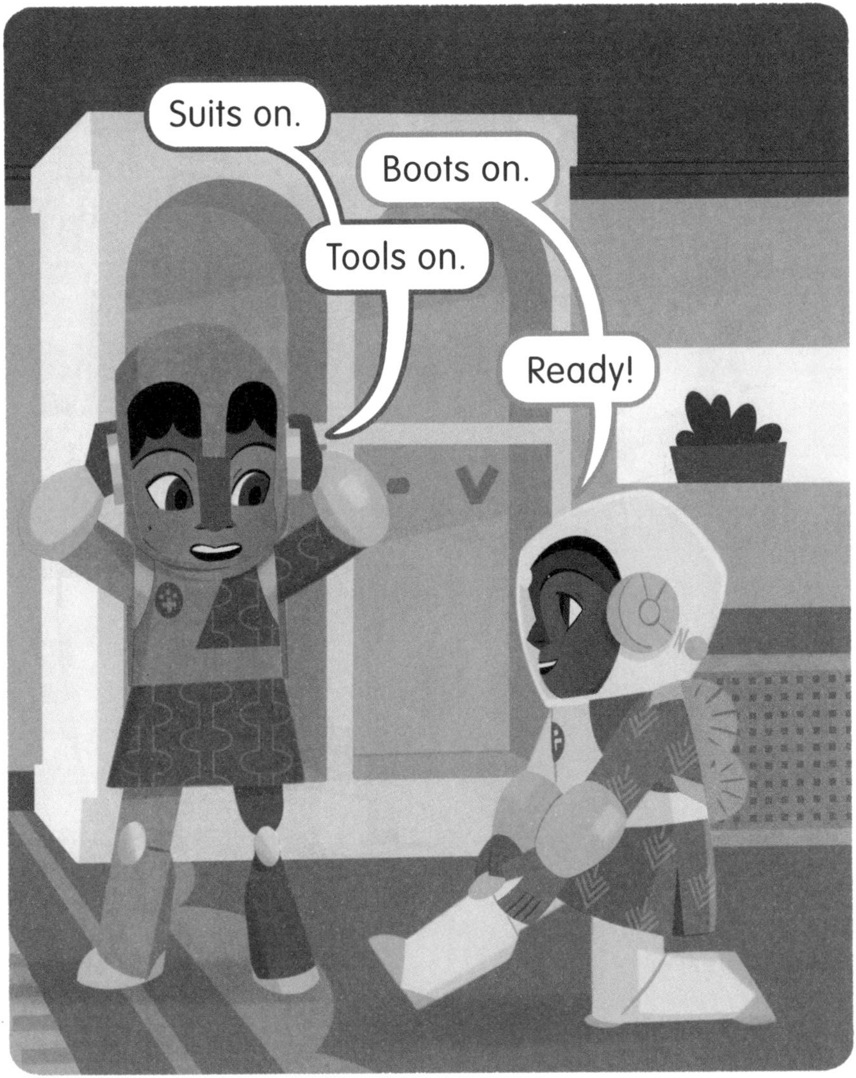
Suits on.
Boots on.
Tools on.
Ready!

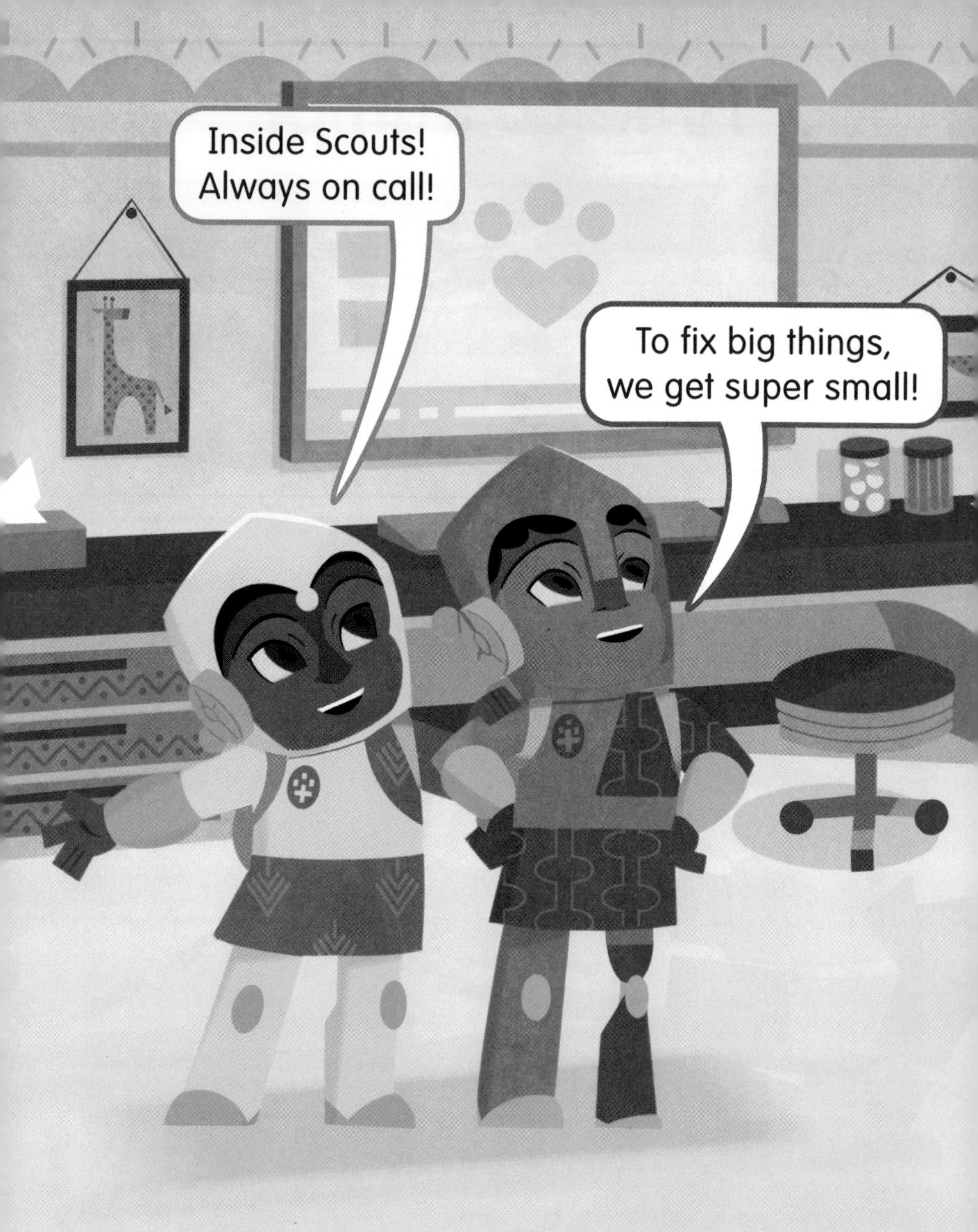
Inside Scouts! Always on call!
To fix big things, we get super small!

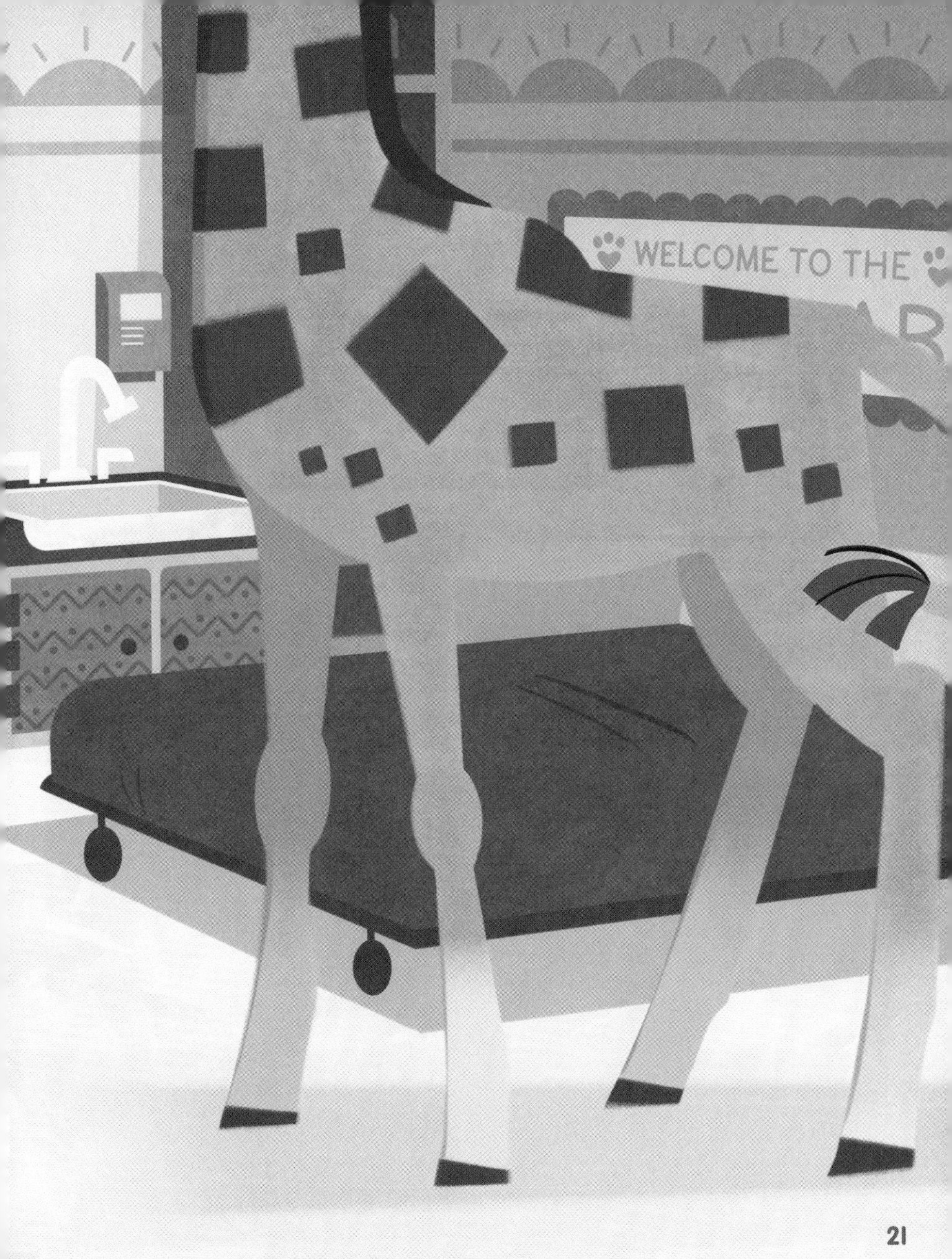
WELCOME TO THE

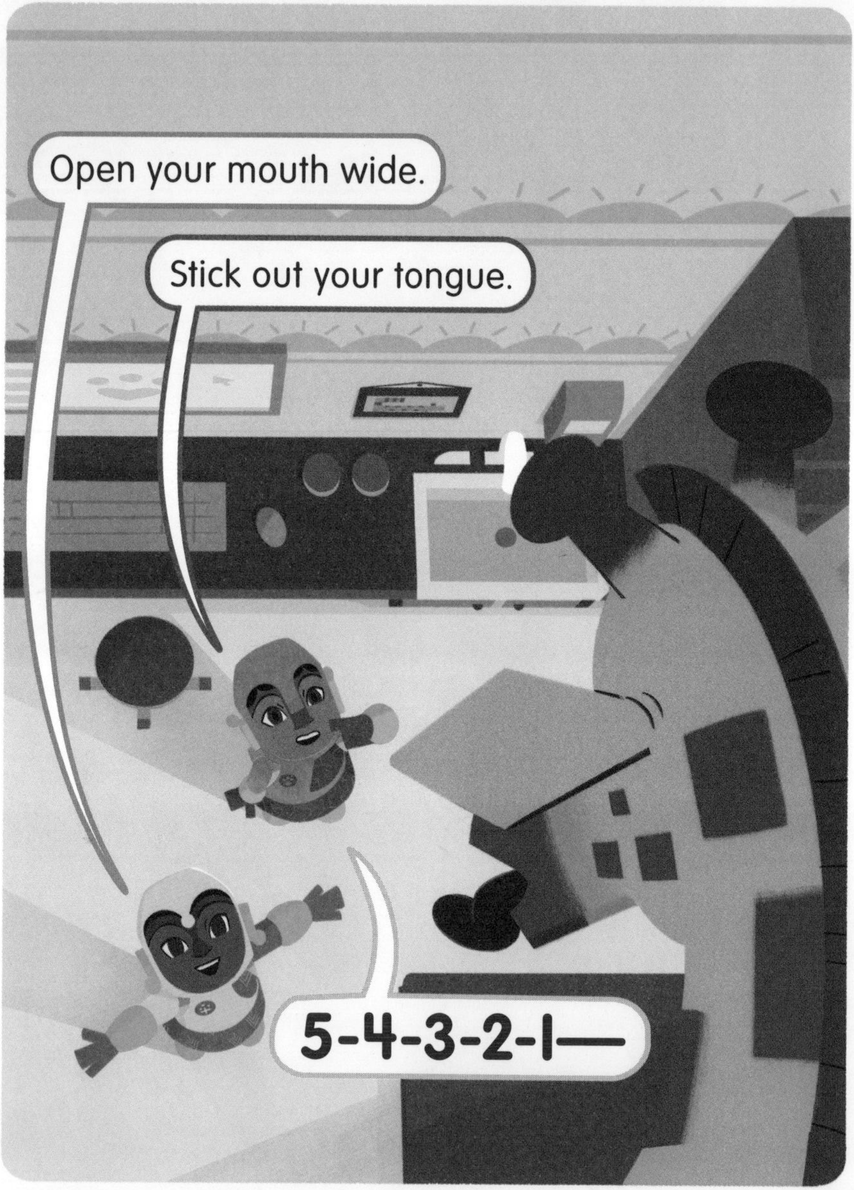
Open your mouth wide.
Stick out your tongue.
5-4-3-2-1—

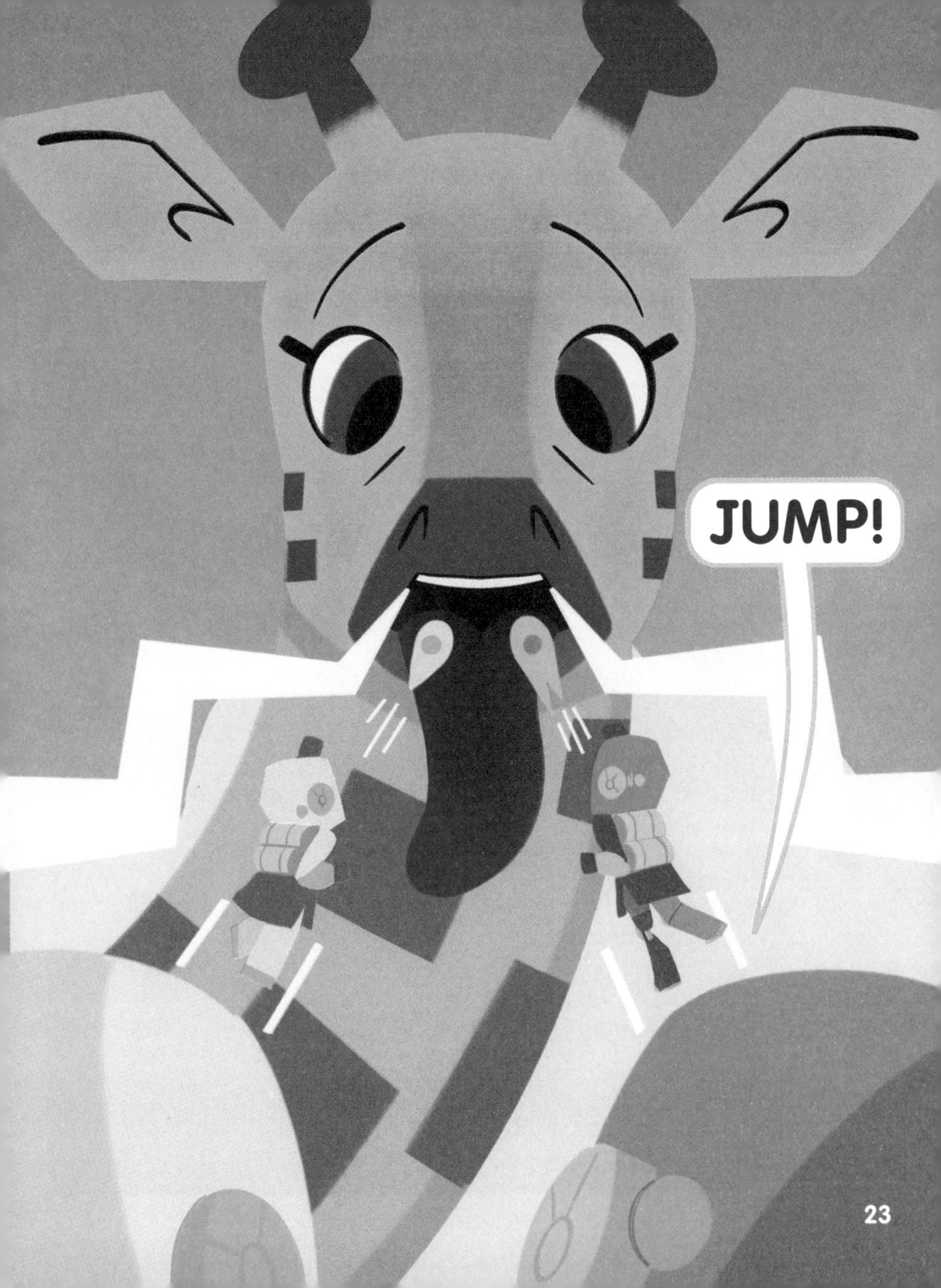
JUMP!

We Can Do This

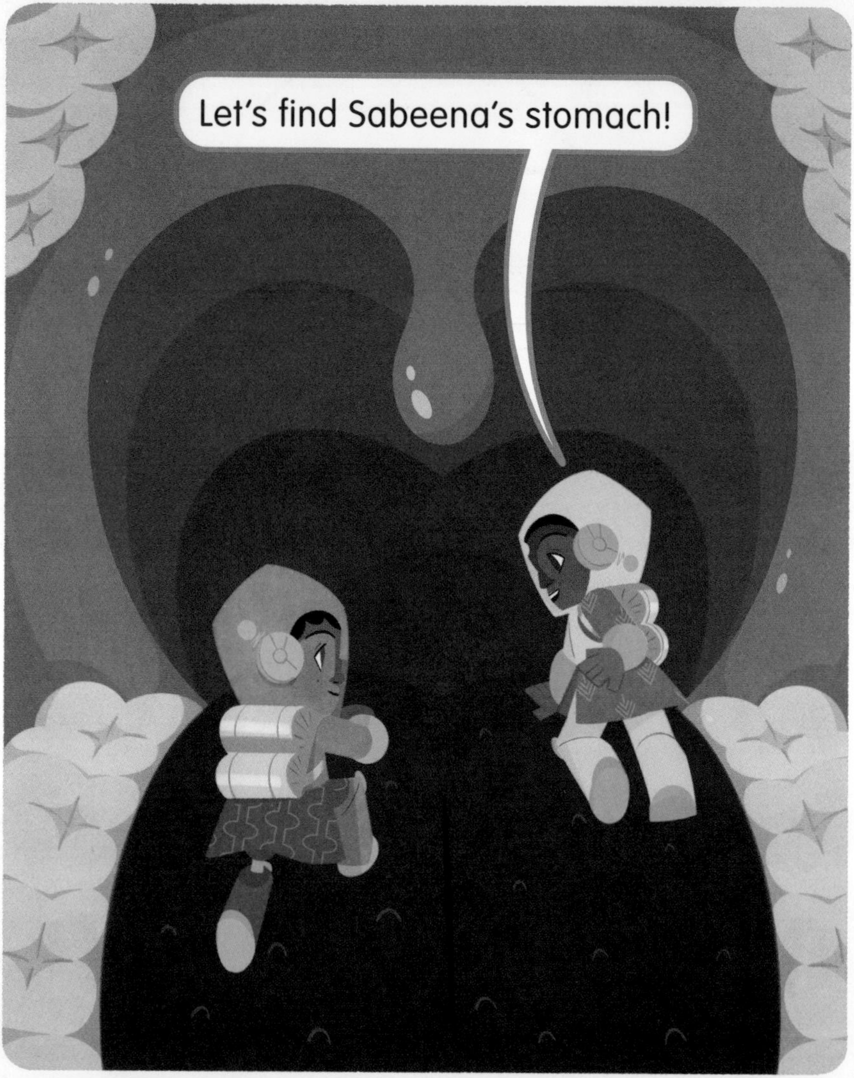
Let's find Sabeena's stomach!

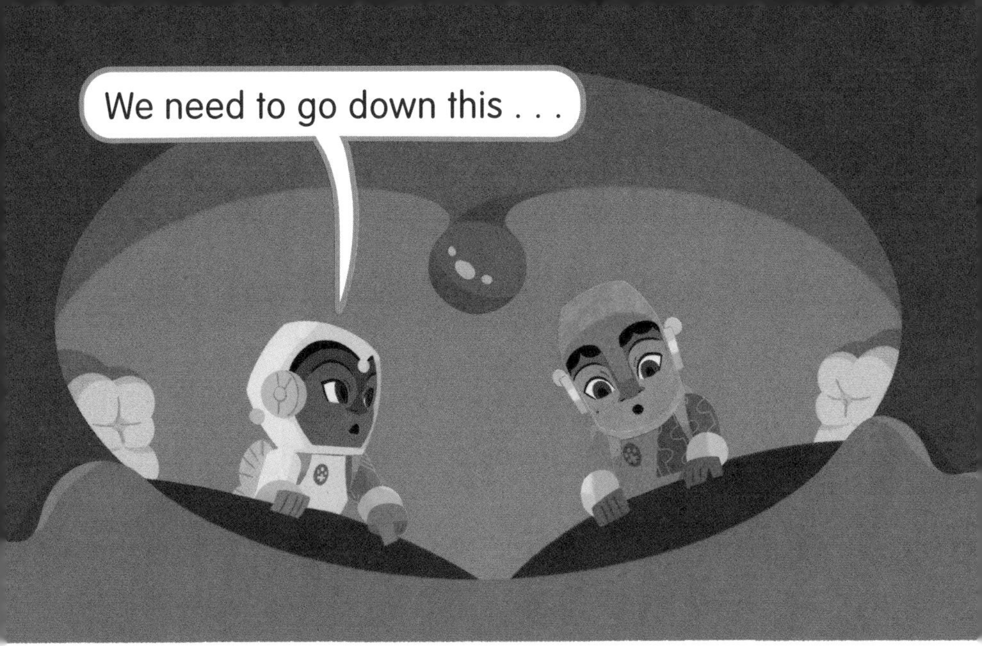
We need to go down this . . .

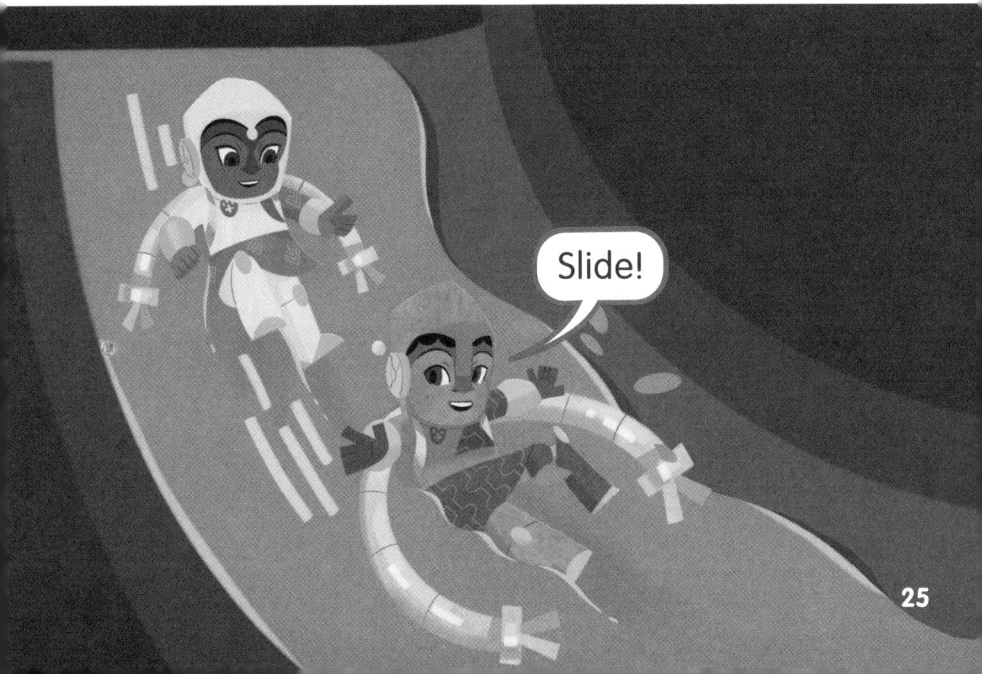
Slide!

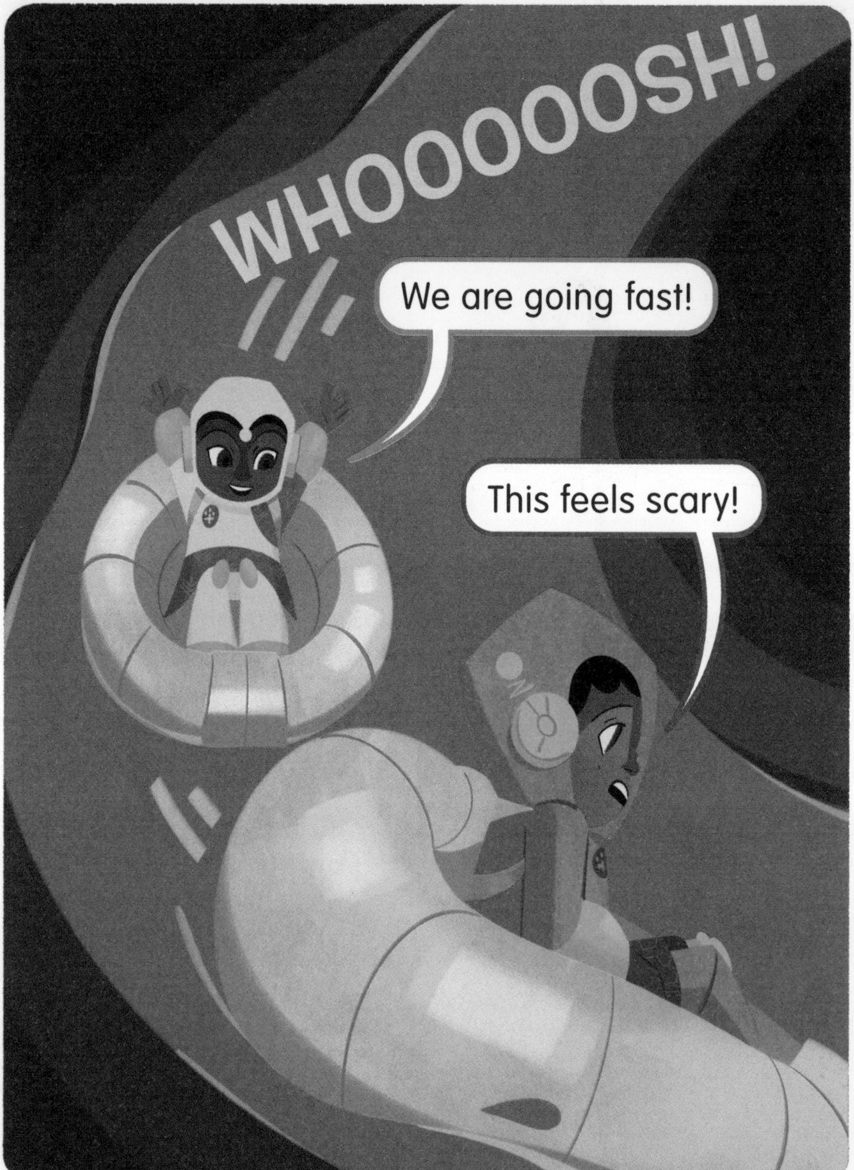
WHOOOOOOSH!
We are going fast!
This feels scary!

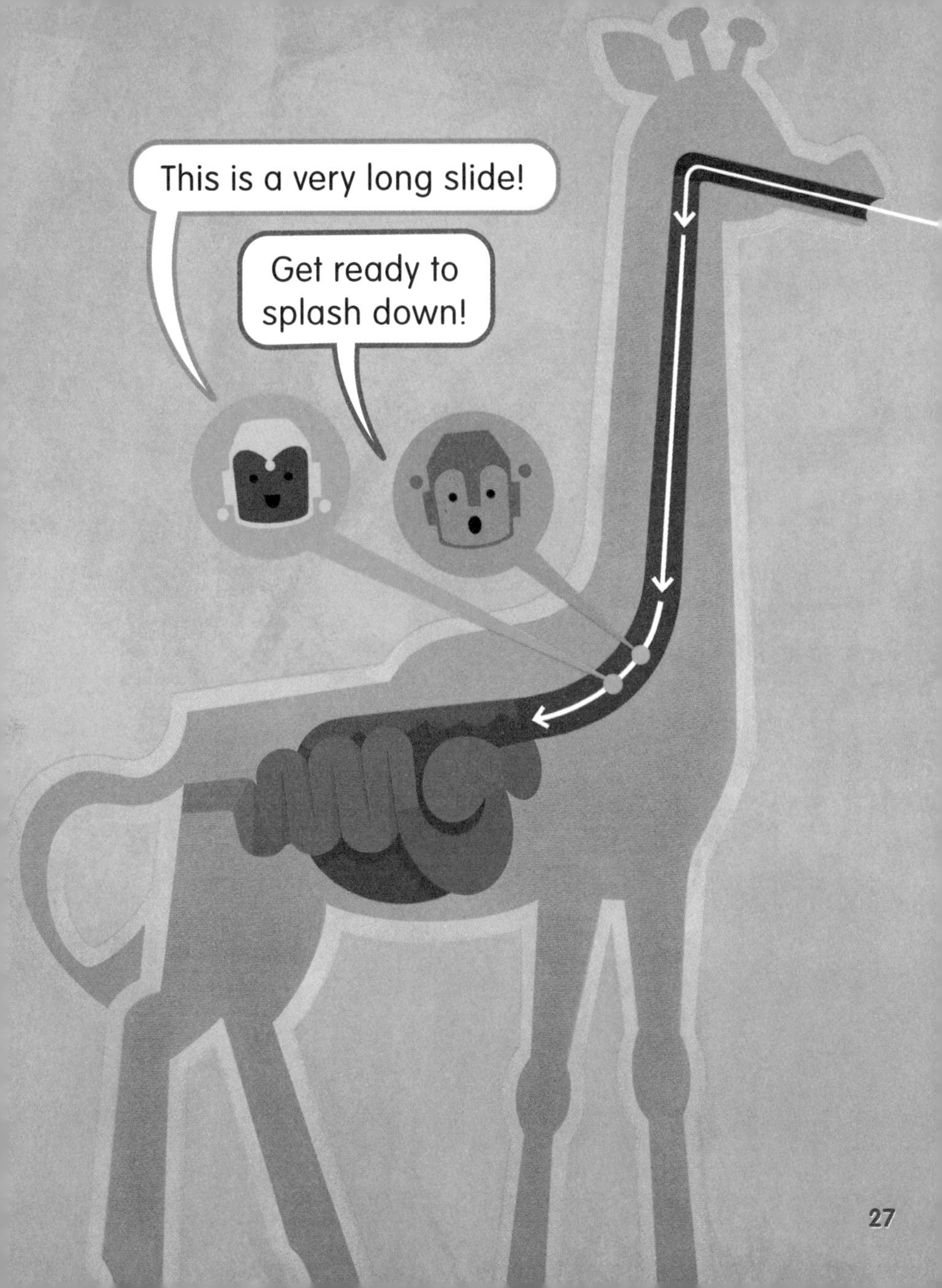
This is a very long slide!
Get ready to splash down!

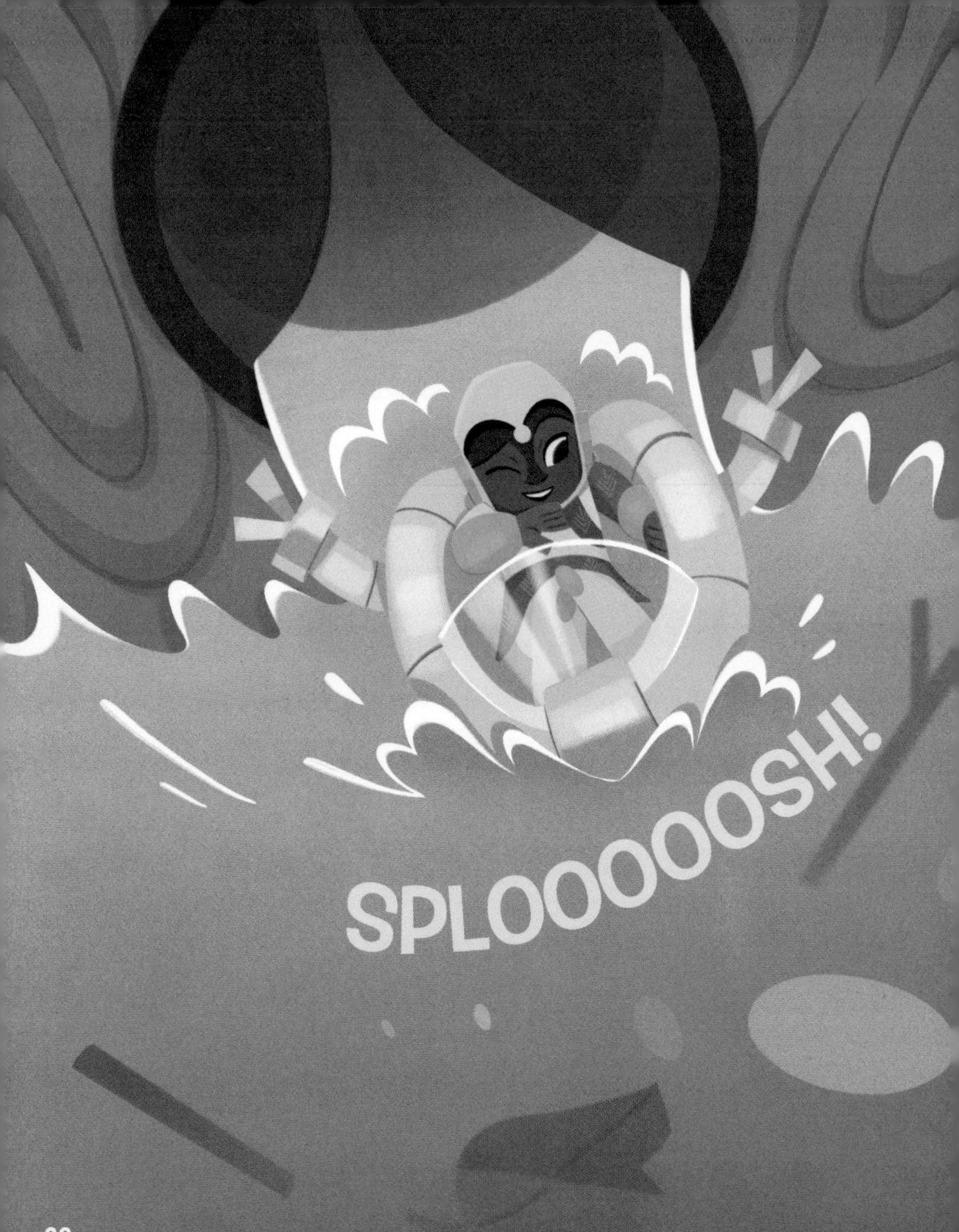
SPLOOOOOOSH!

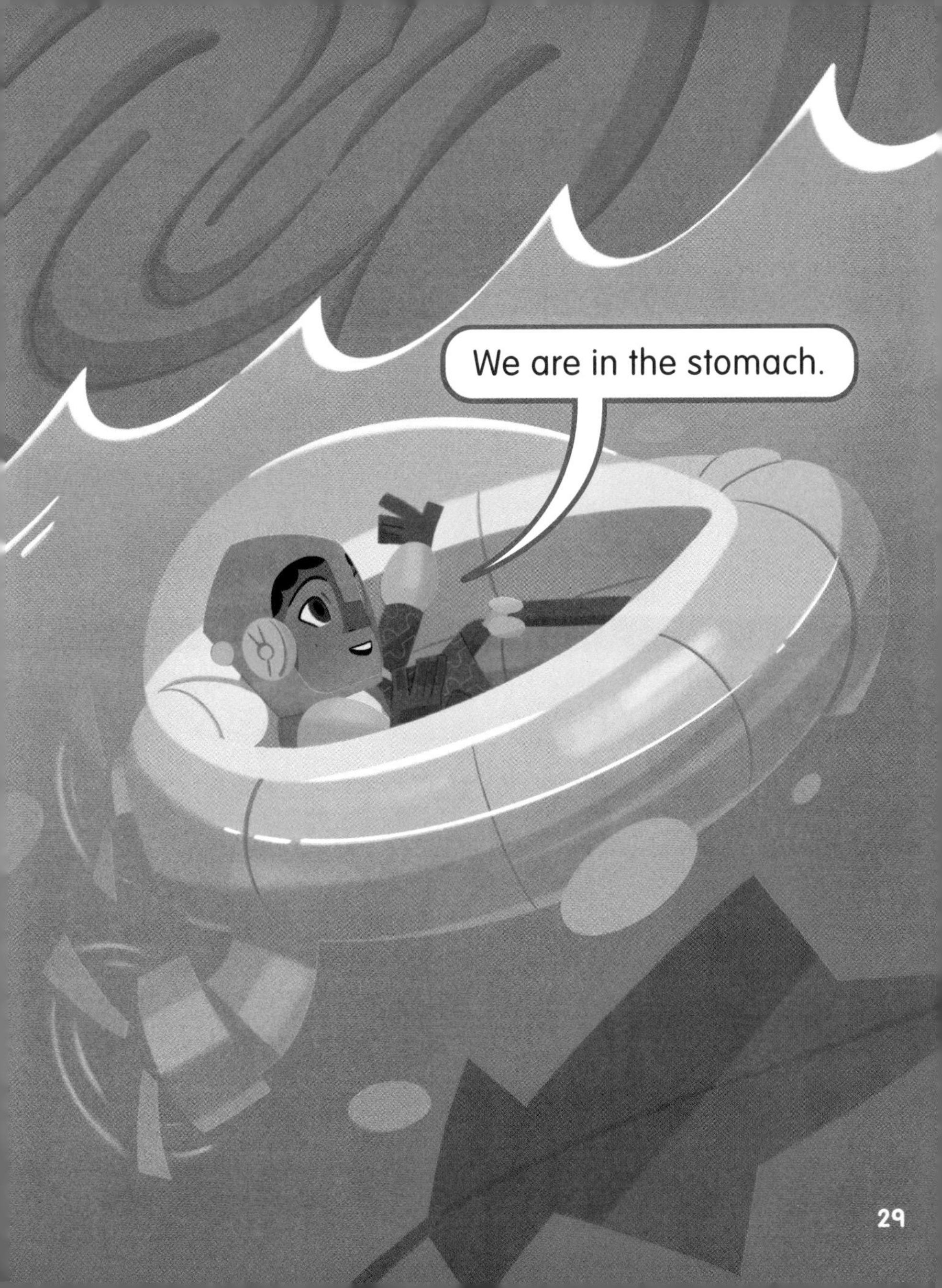
We are in the stomach.

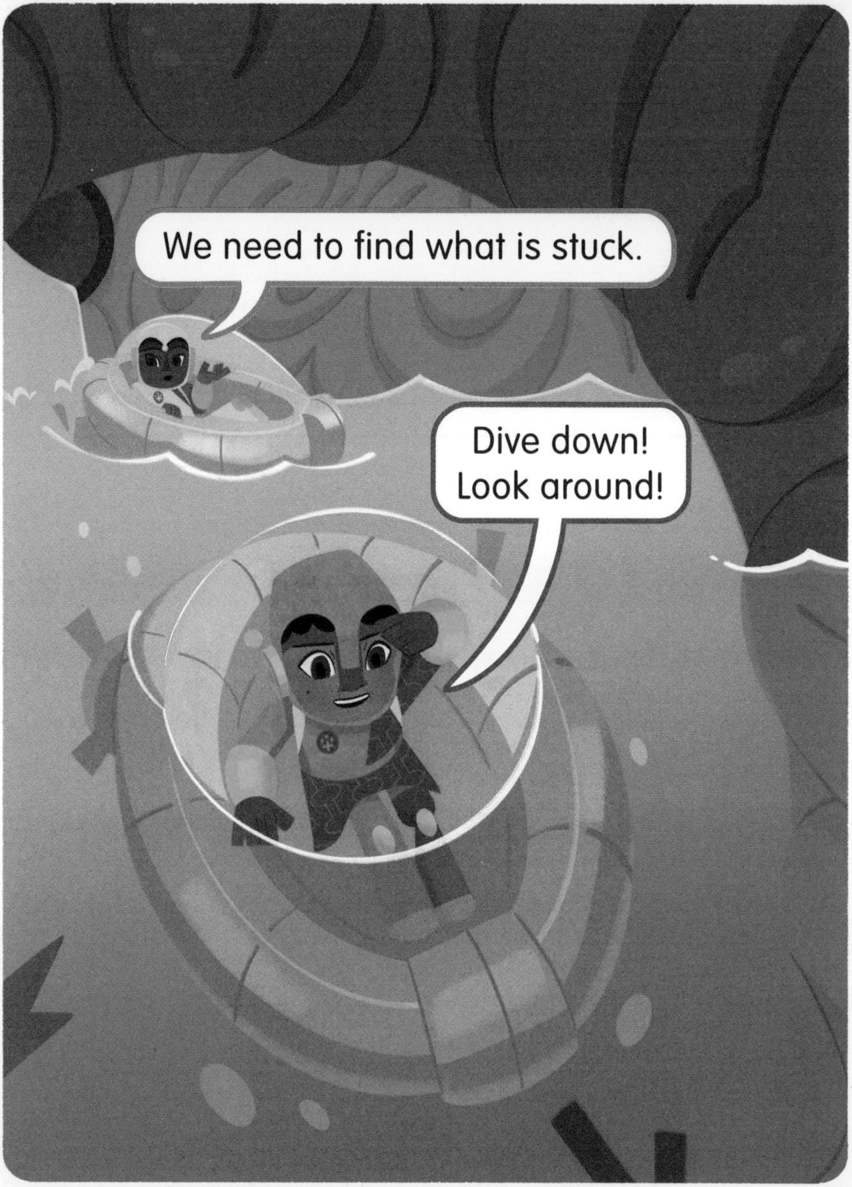
We need to find what is stuck.
Dive down! Look around!

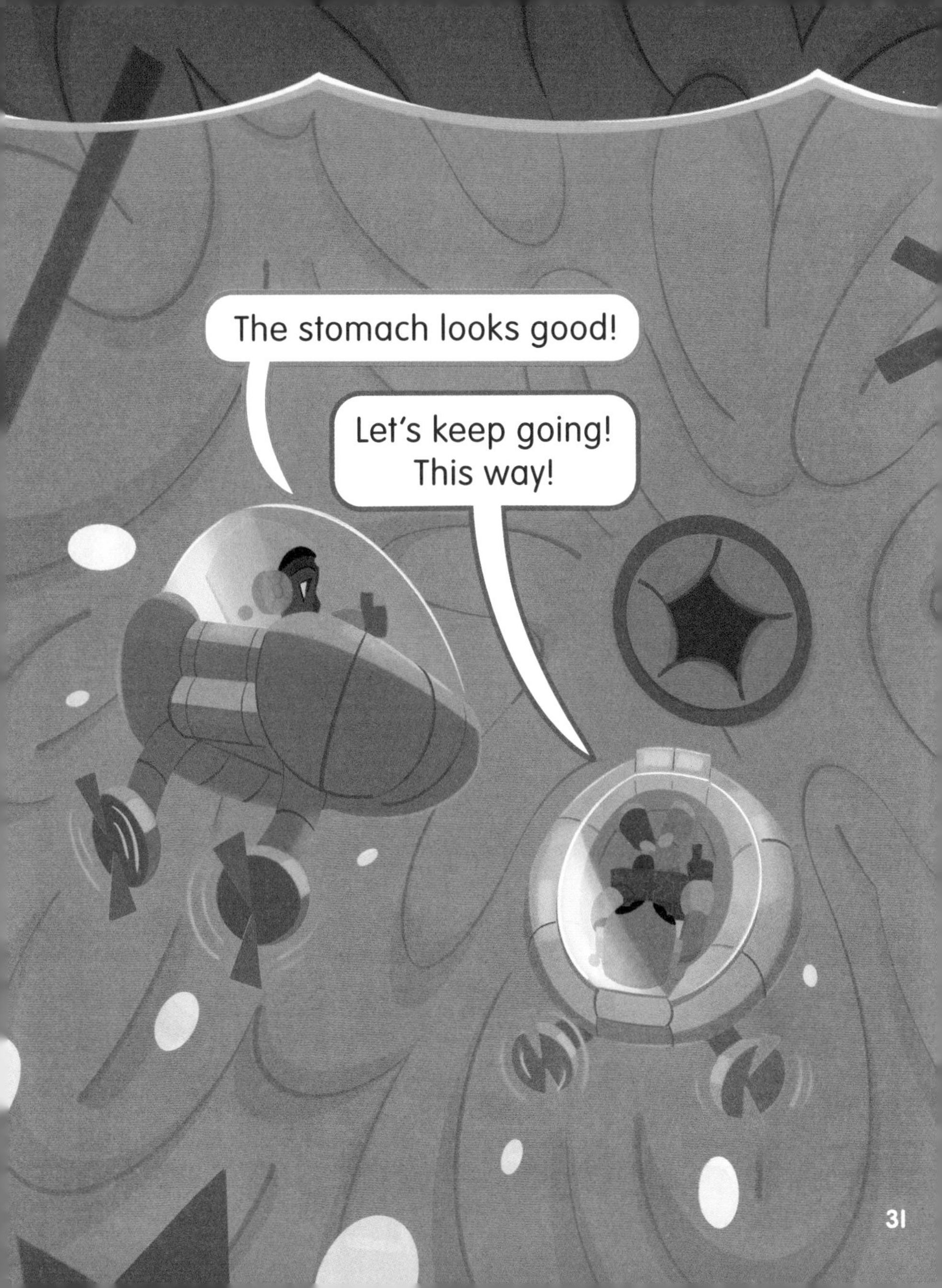
The stomach looks good!
Let's keep going! This way!

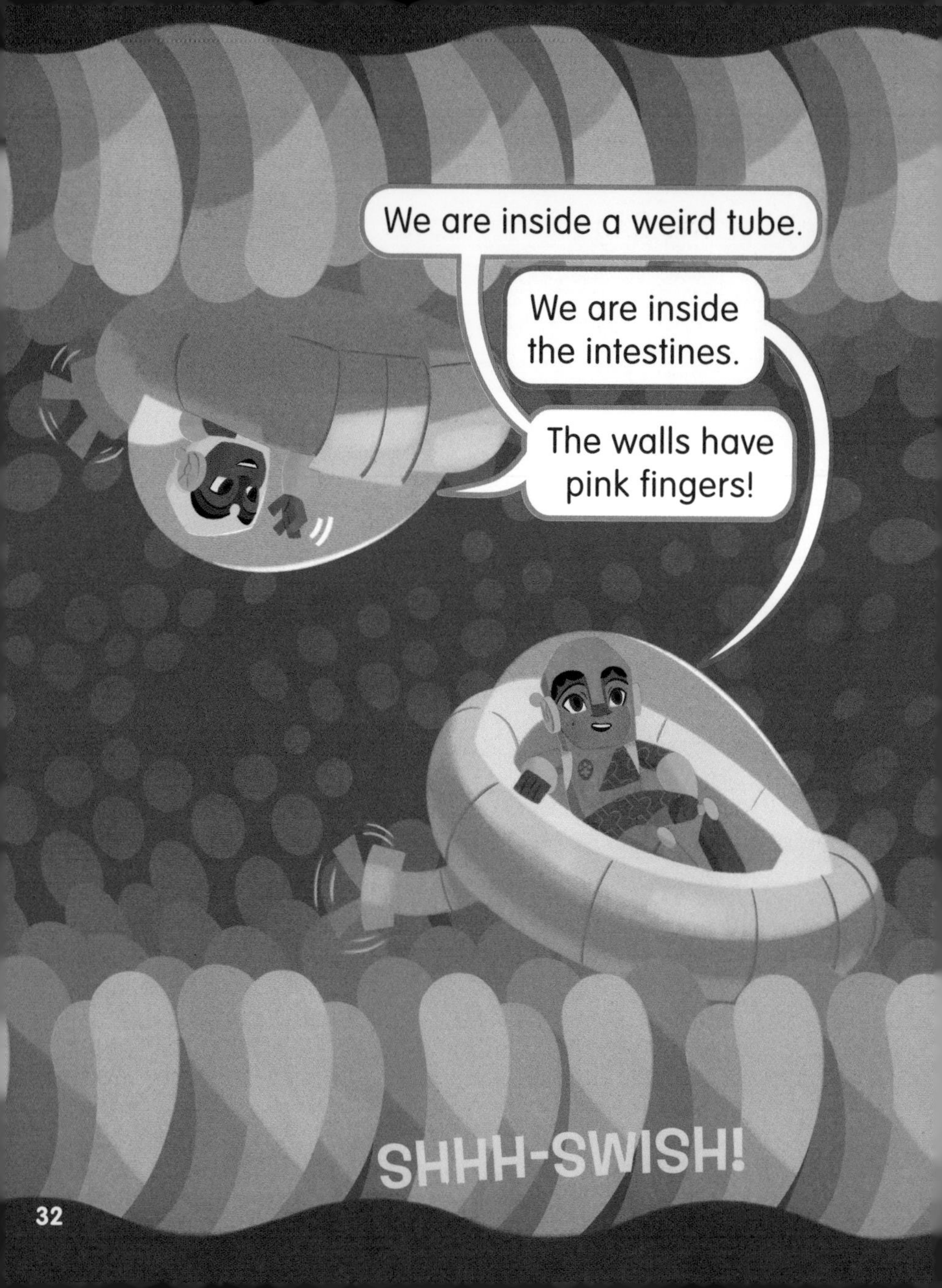
We are inside a weird tube.
We are inside the intestines.
The walls have pink fingers!
SHHH-SWISH!

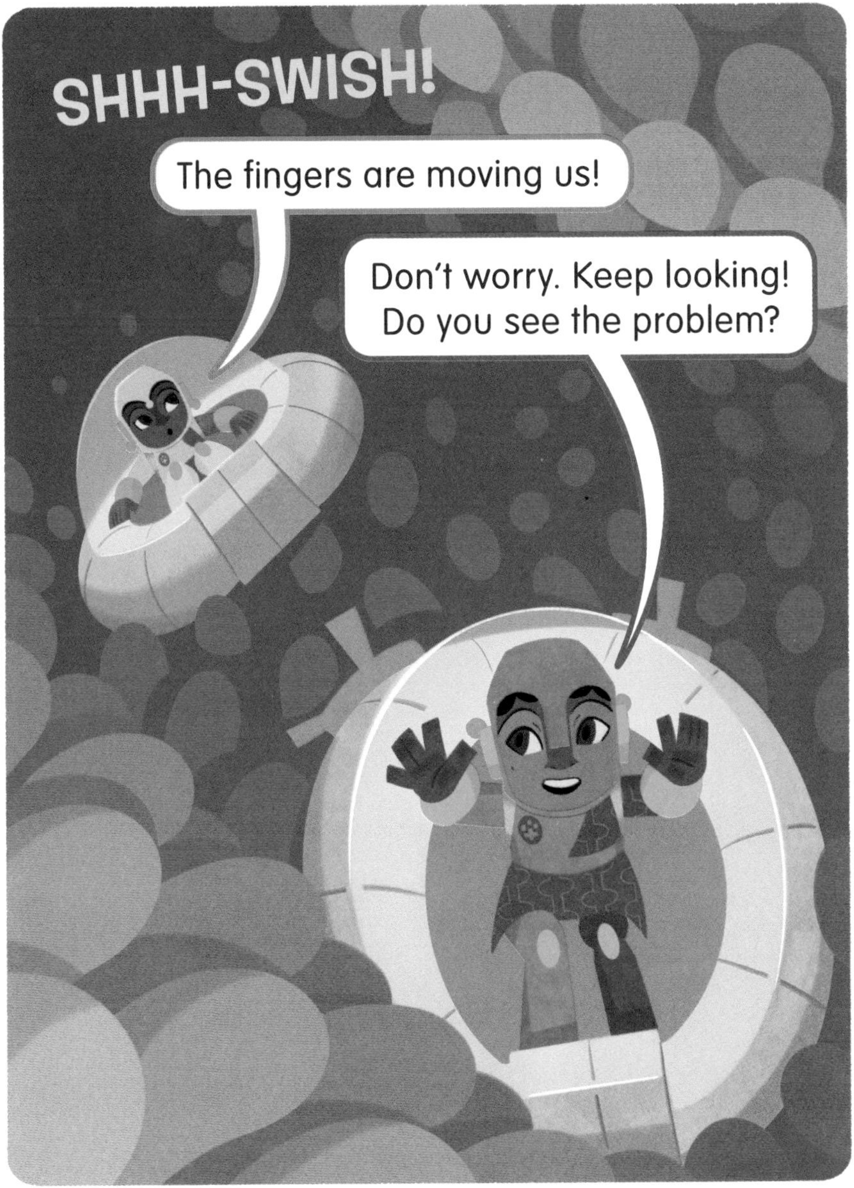
SHHH-SWISH!
The fingers are moving us!
Don't worry. Keep looking! Do you see the problem?

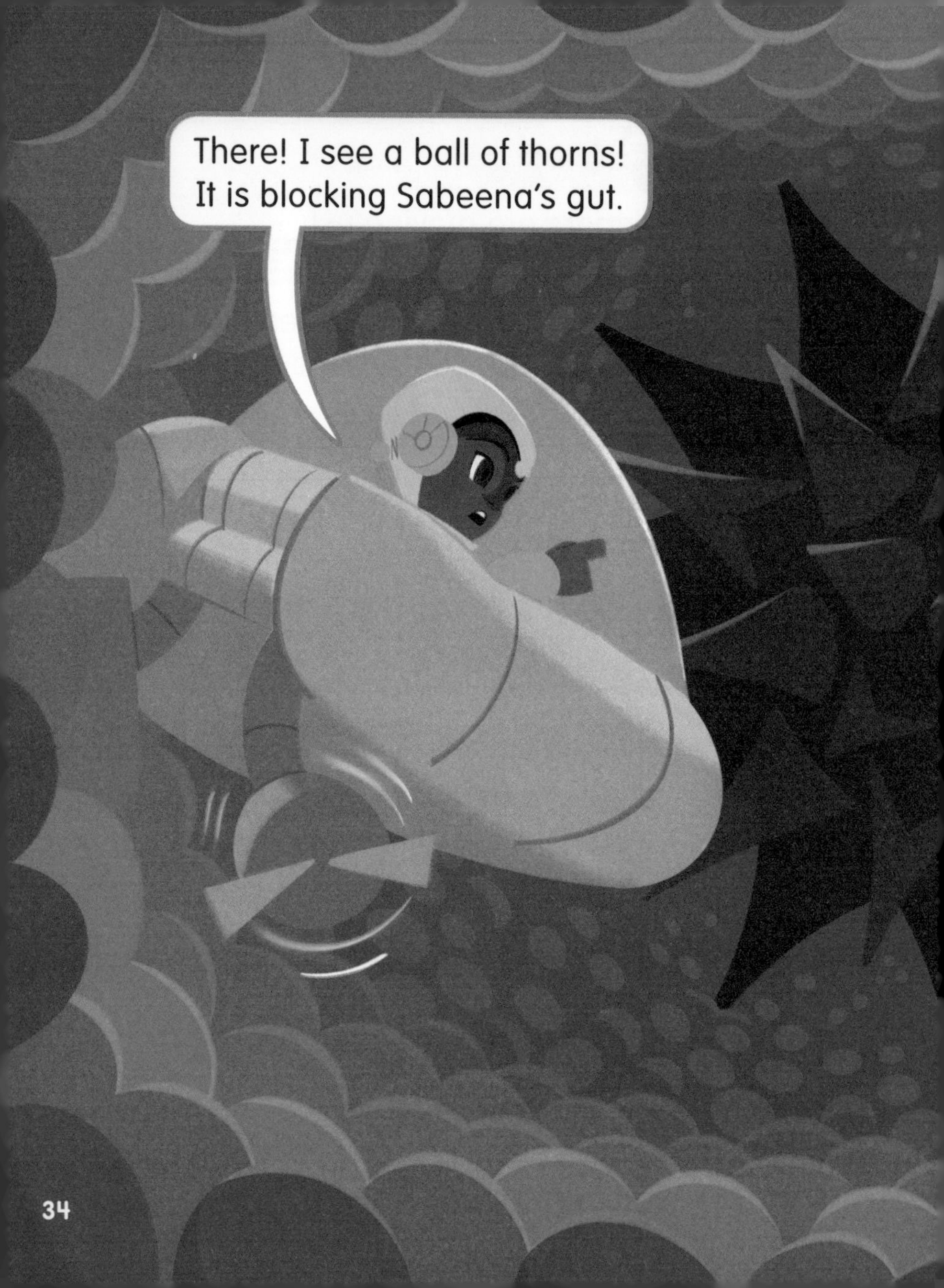
There! I see a ball of thorns!
It is blocking Sabeena's gut.

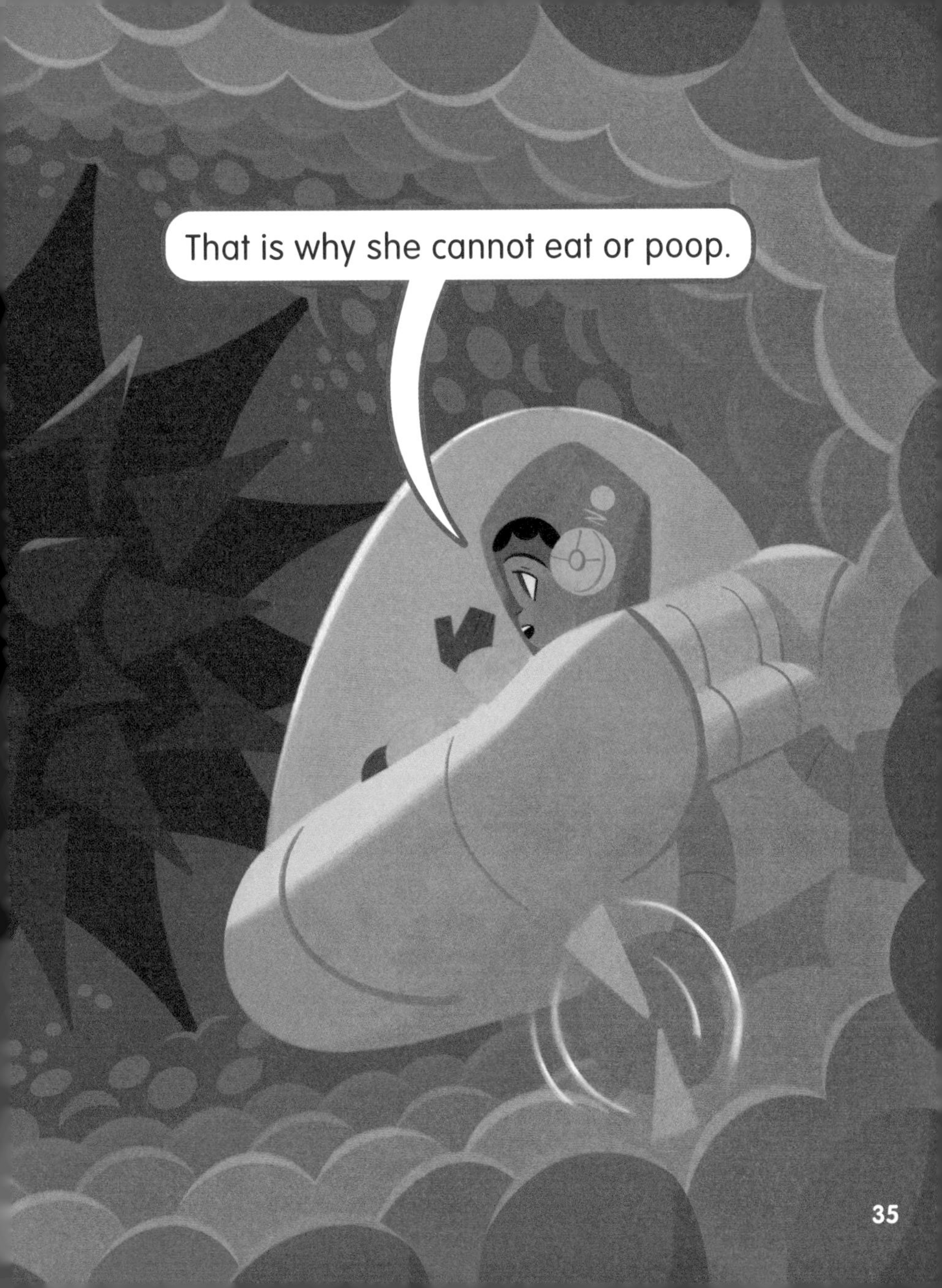
That is why she cannot eat or poop.

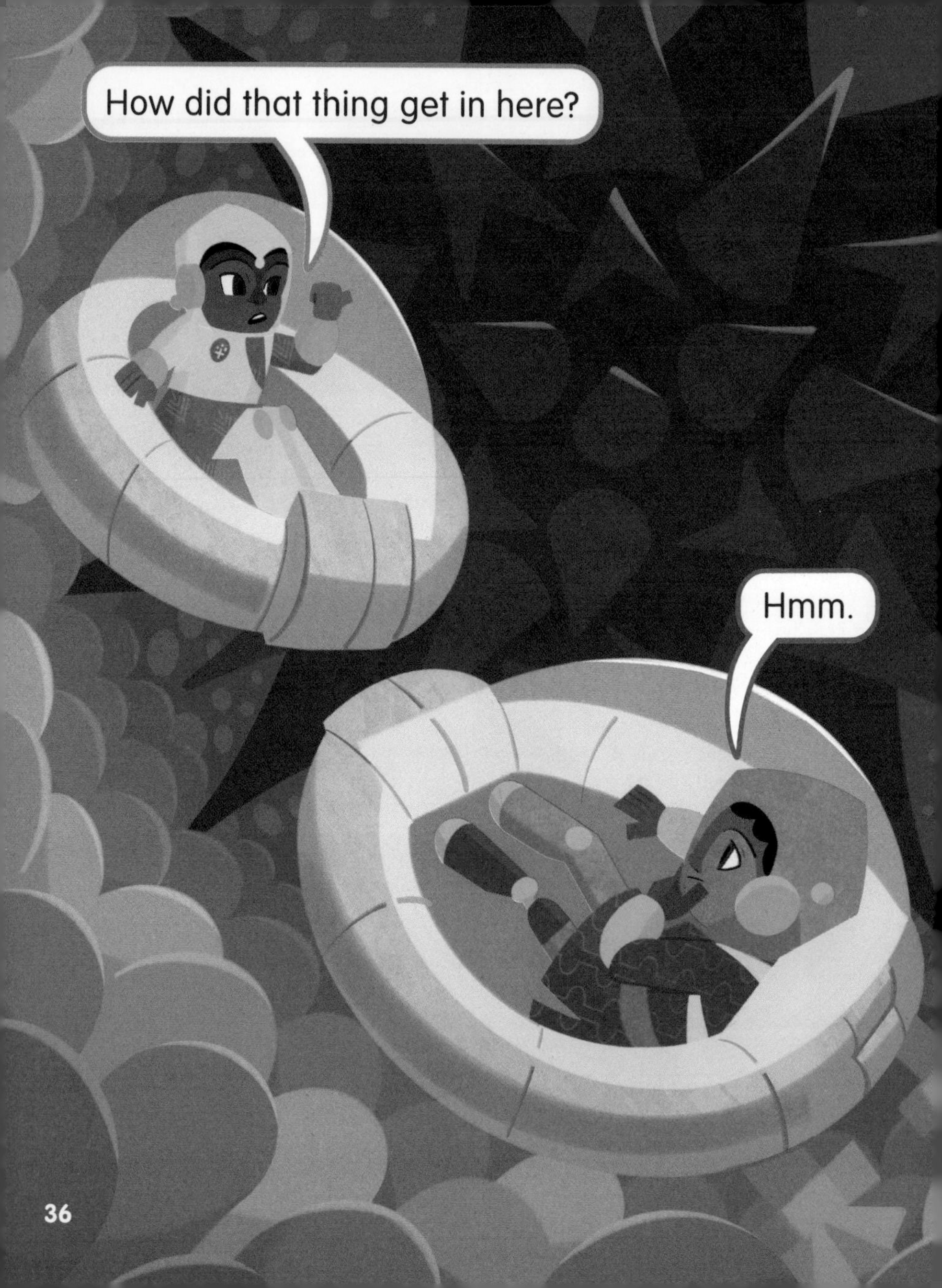
How did that thing get in here?
Hmm.

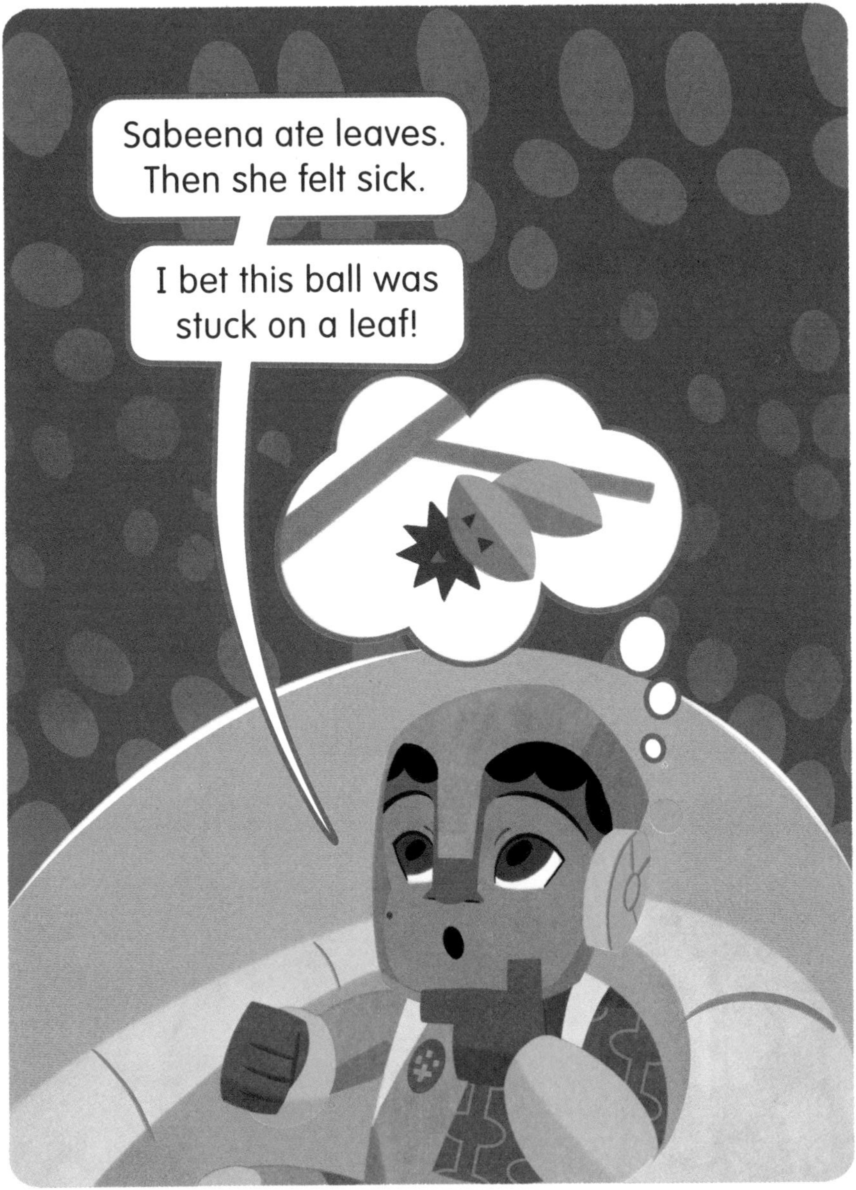
Sabeena ate leaves. Then she felt sick.
I bet this ball was stuck on a leaf!

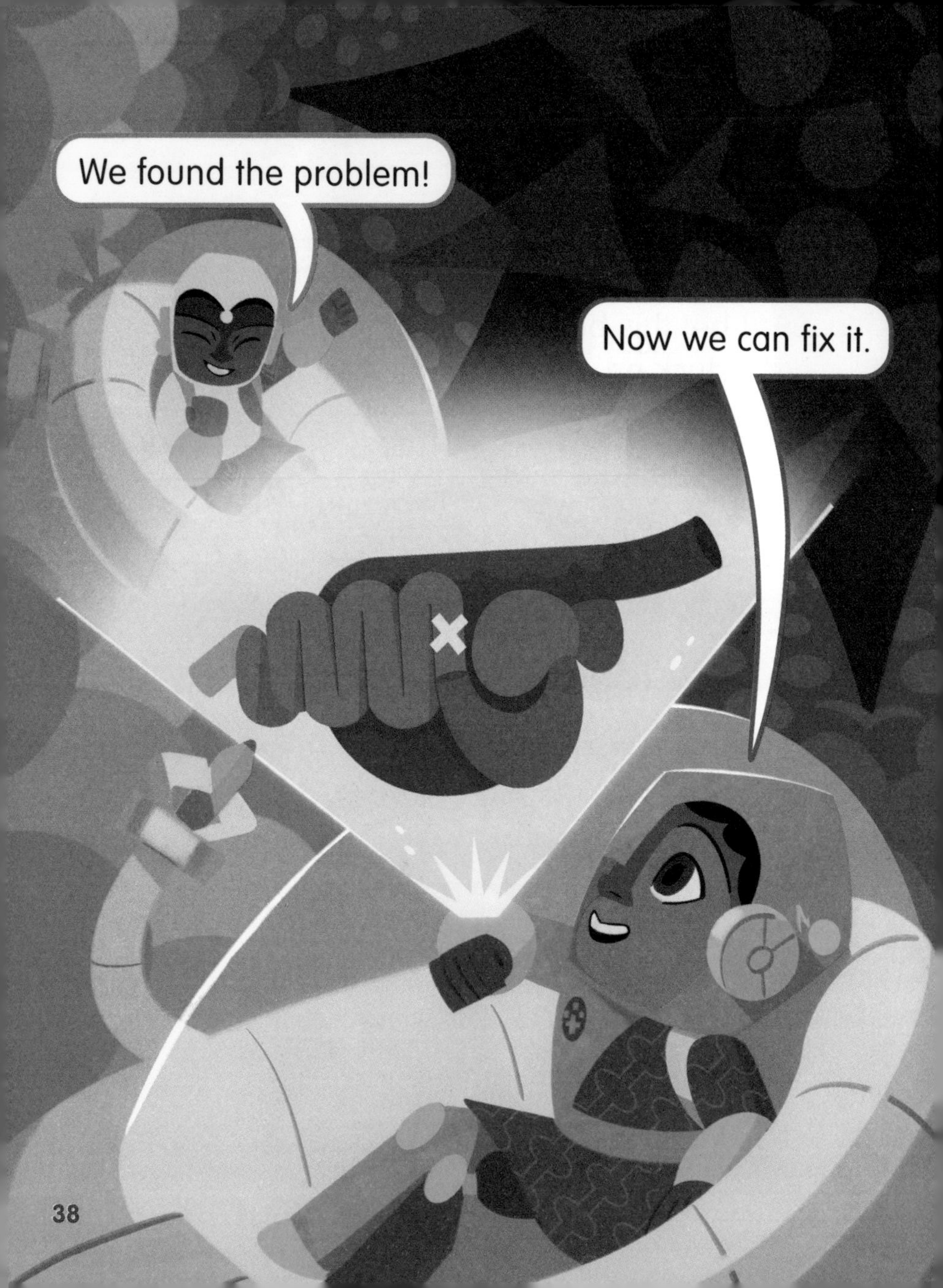
We found the problem!
Now we can fix it.

We Crack It!

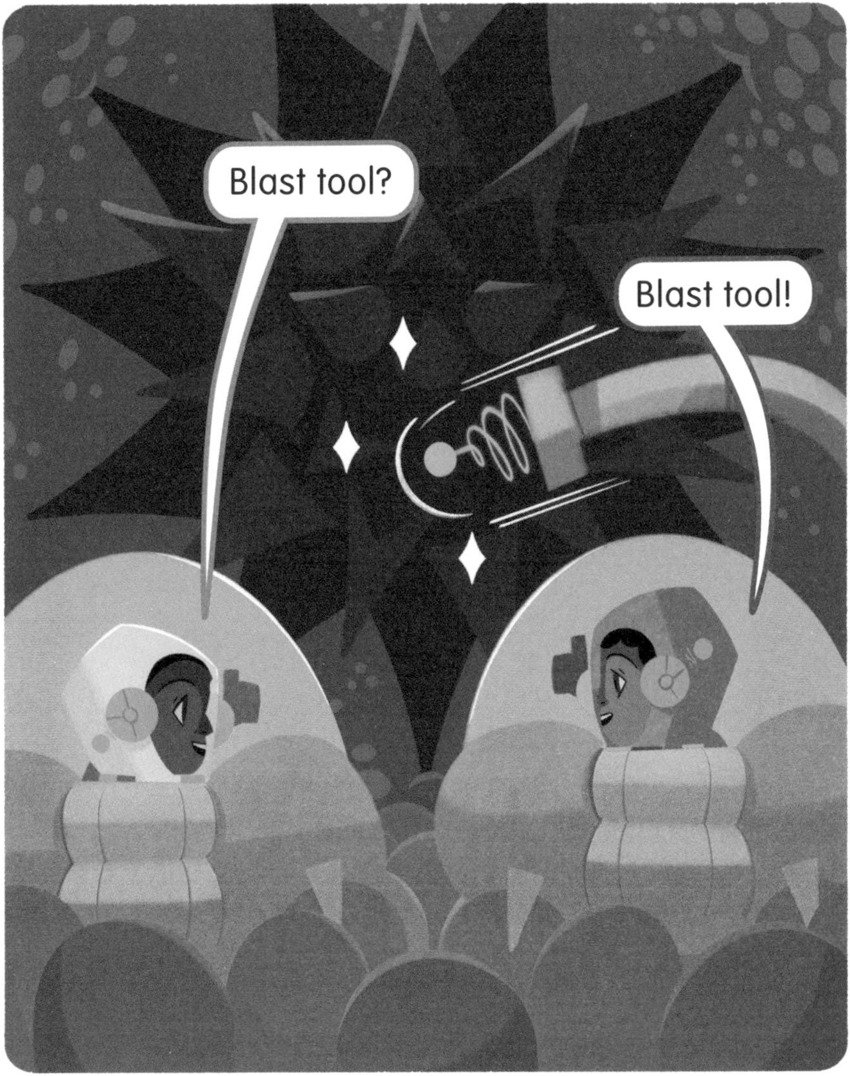
Blast tool?
Blast tool!

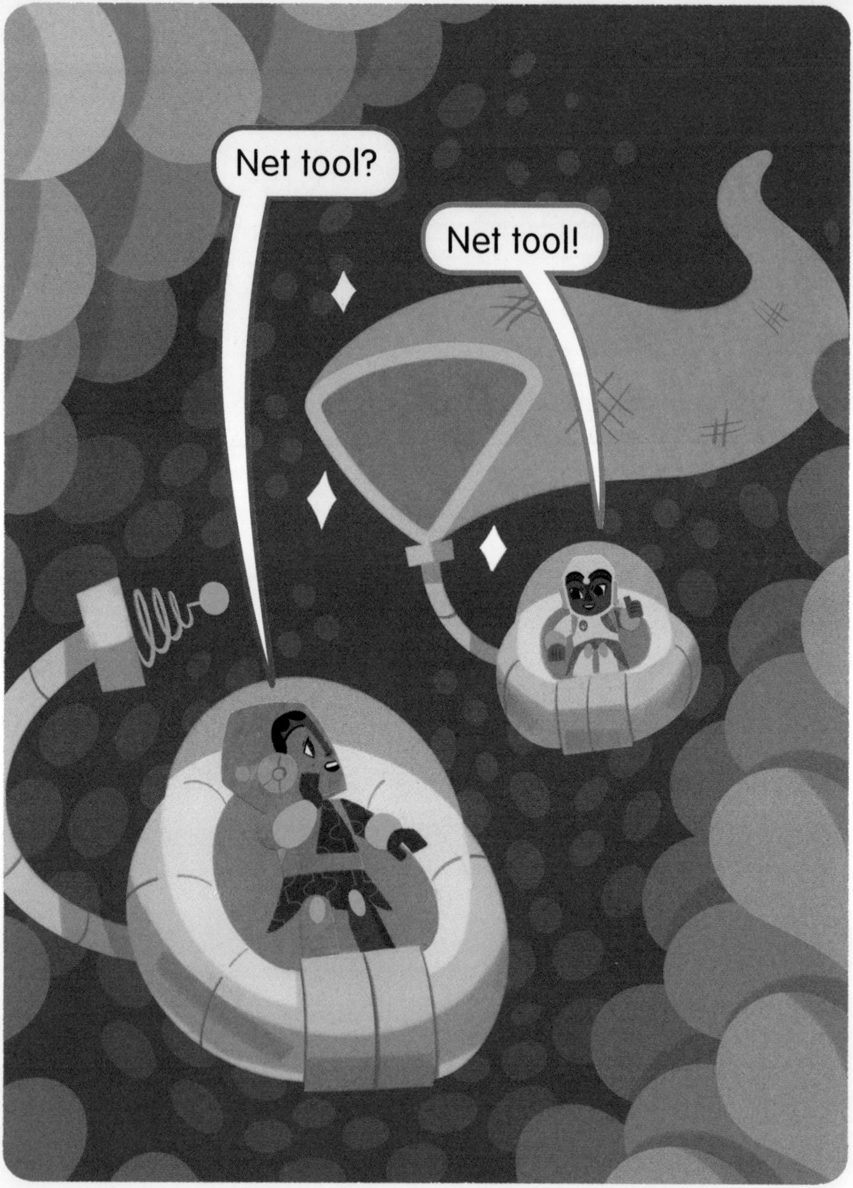
Net tool?
Net tool!

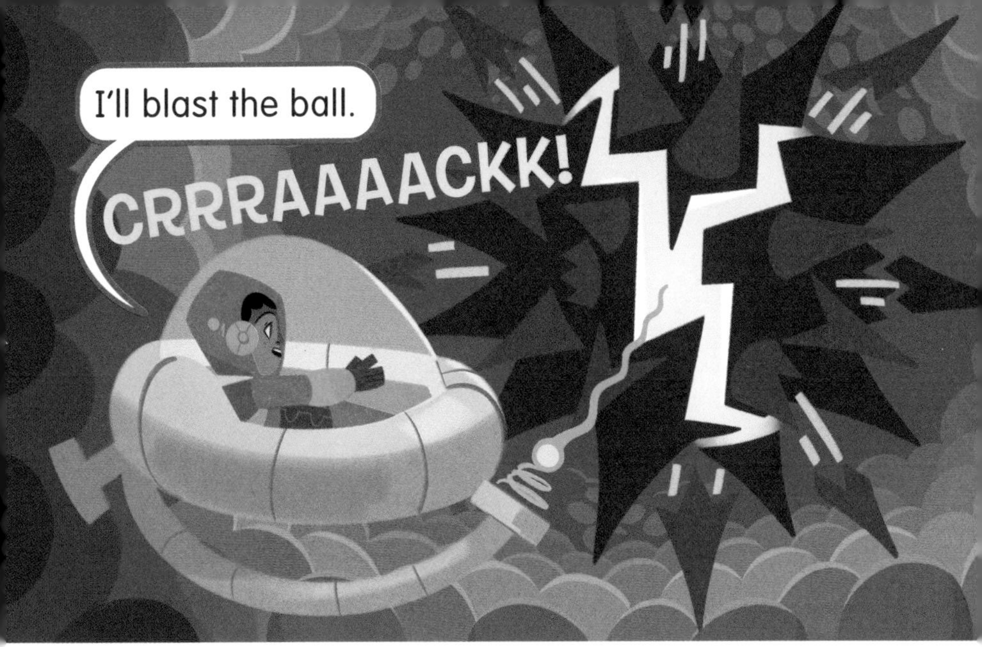
I'll blast the ball.
CRRRAAAACKK!

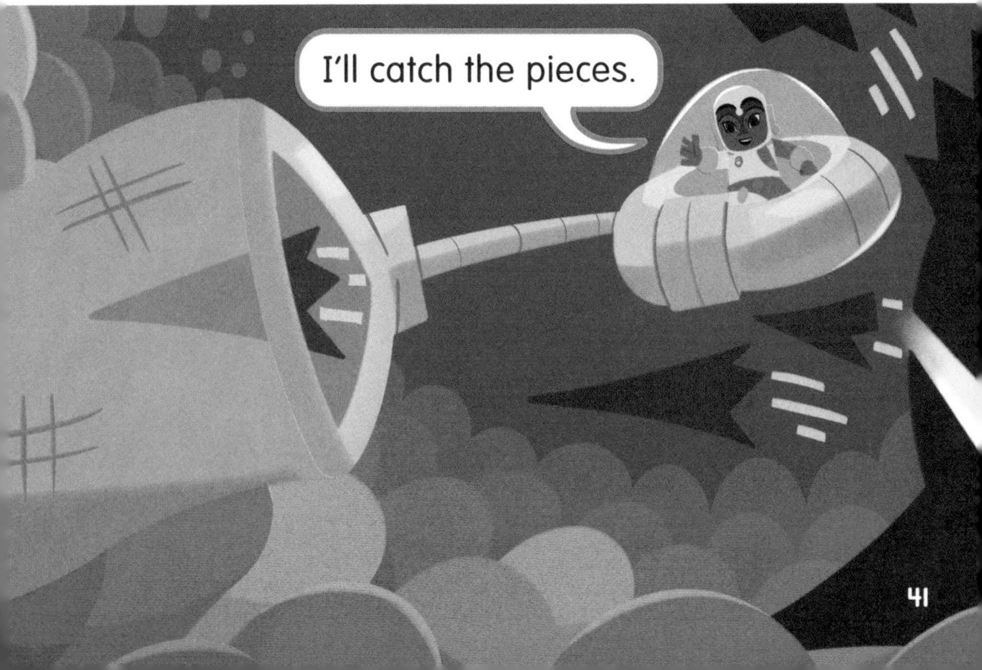
I'll catch the pieces.

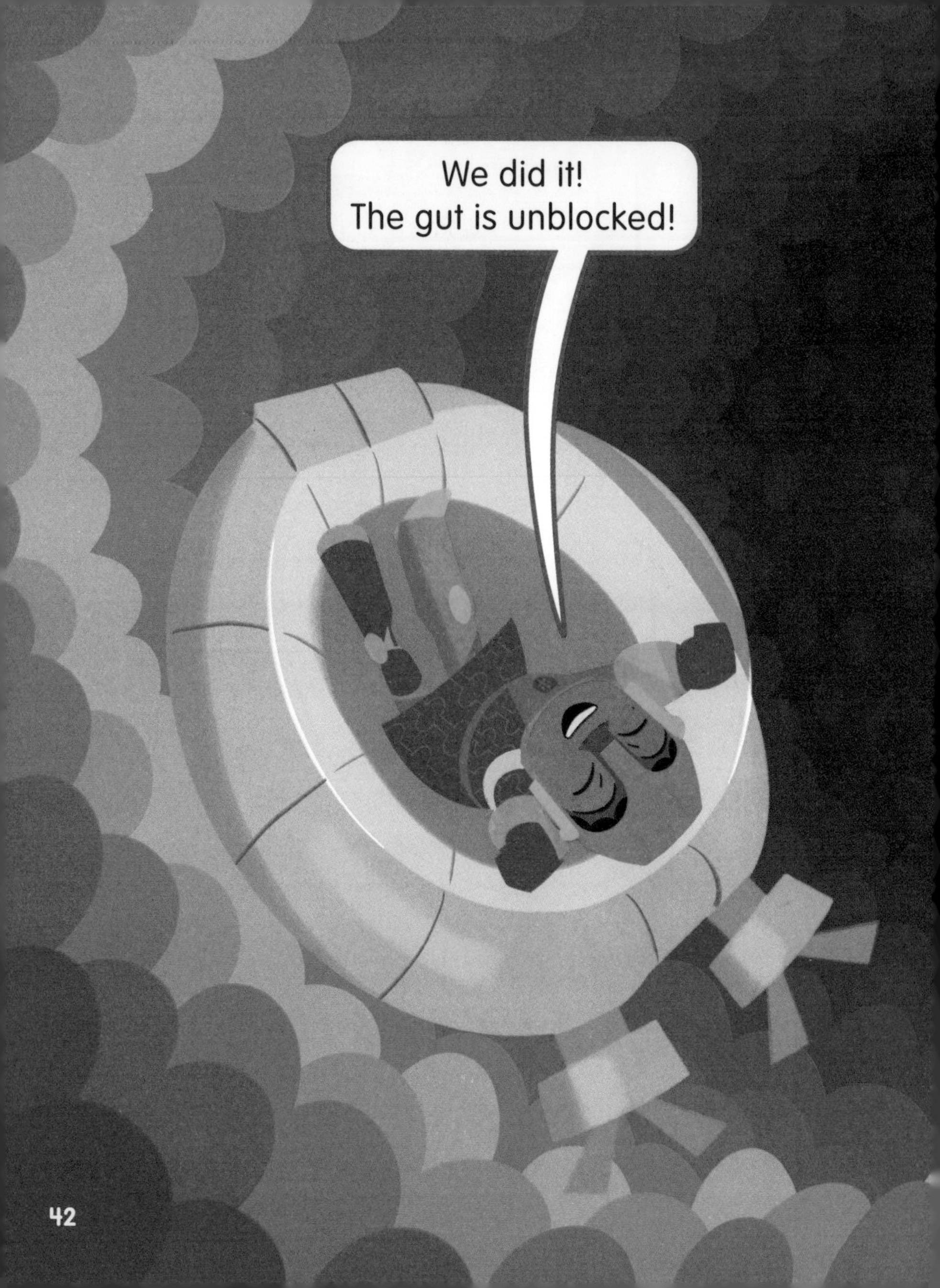
We did it!
The gut is unblocked!

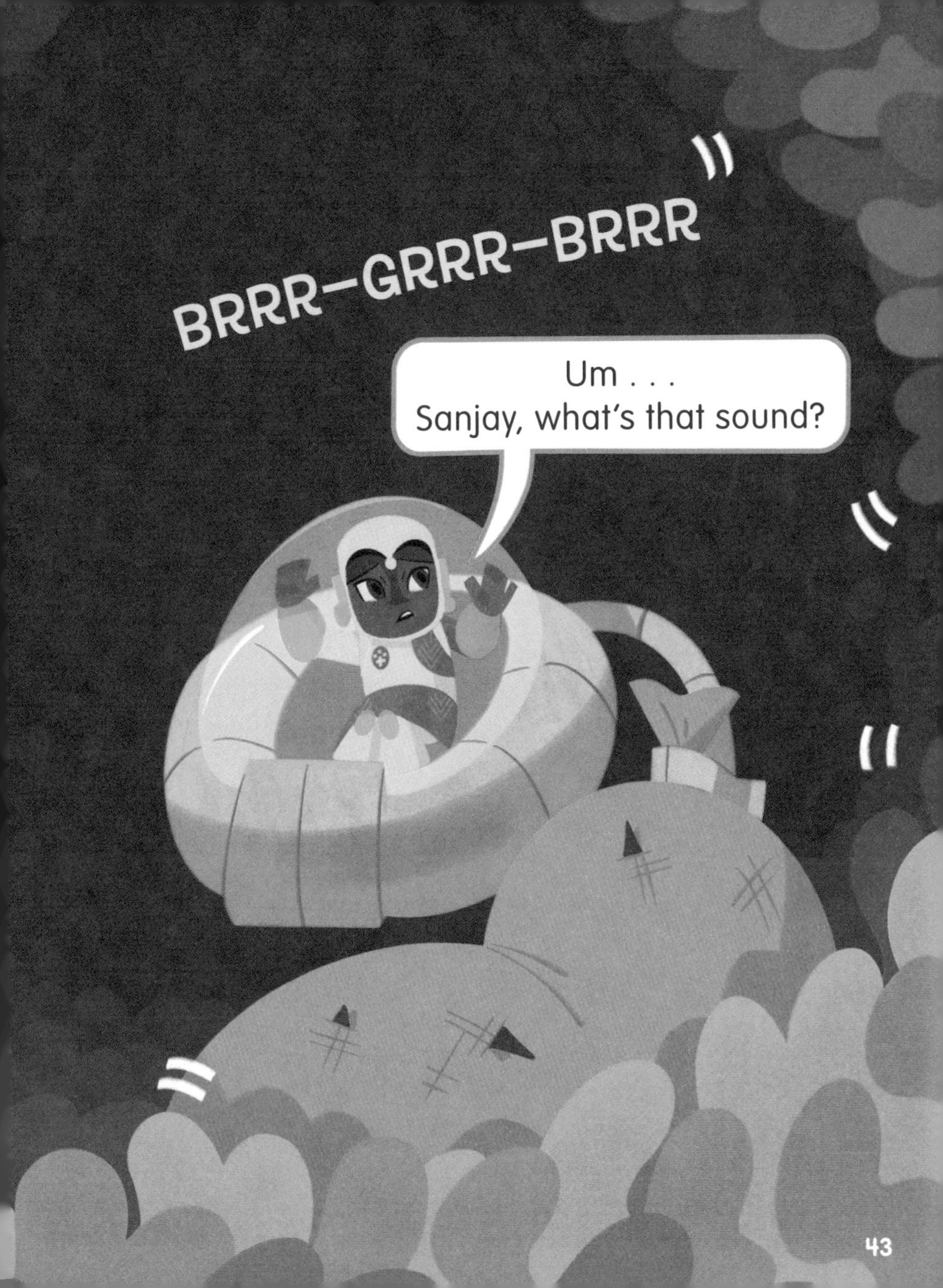
BRRR–GRRR–BRRR
Um . . .
Sanjay, what's that sound?

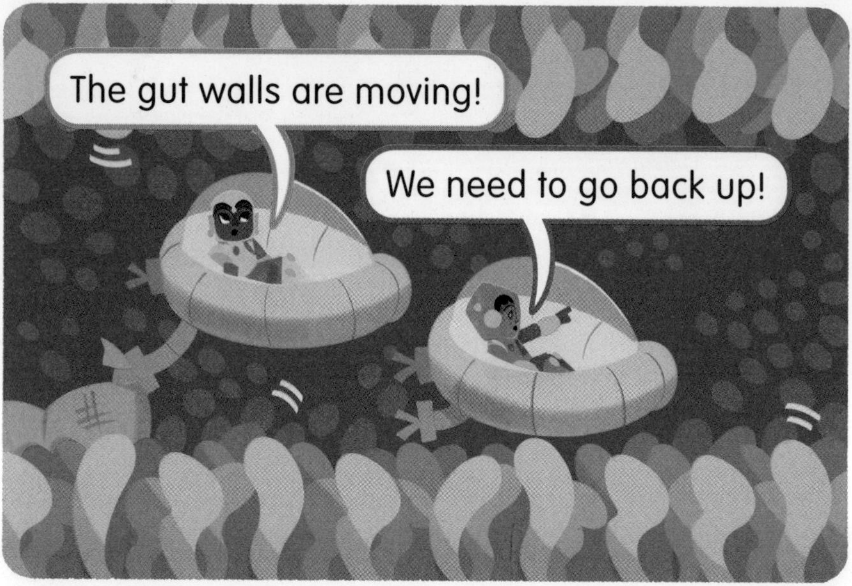
The gut walls are moving!
We need to go back up!

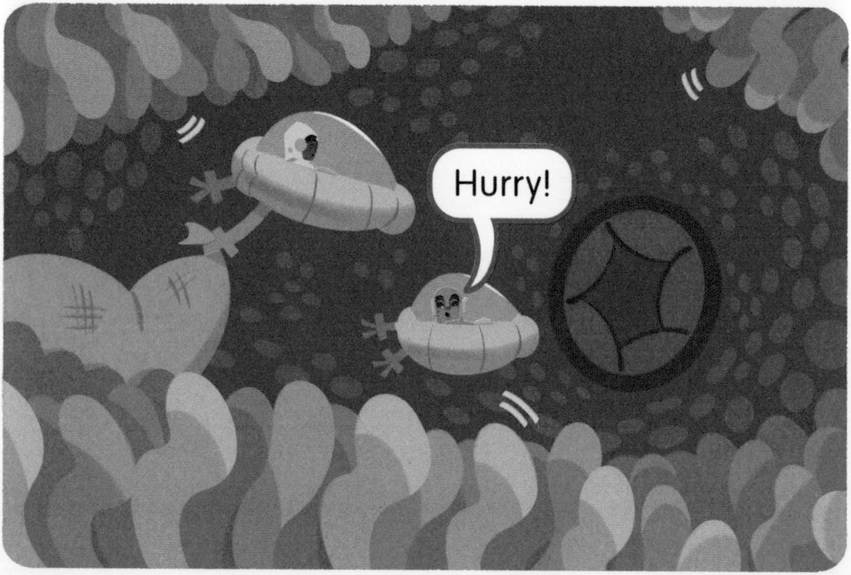
Hurry!

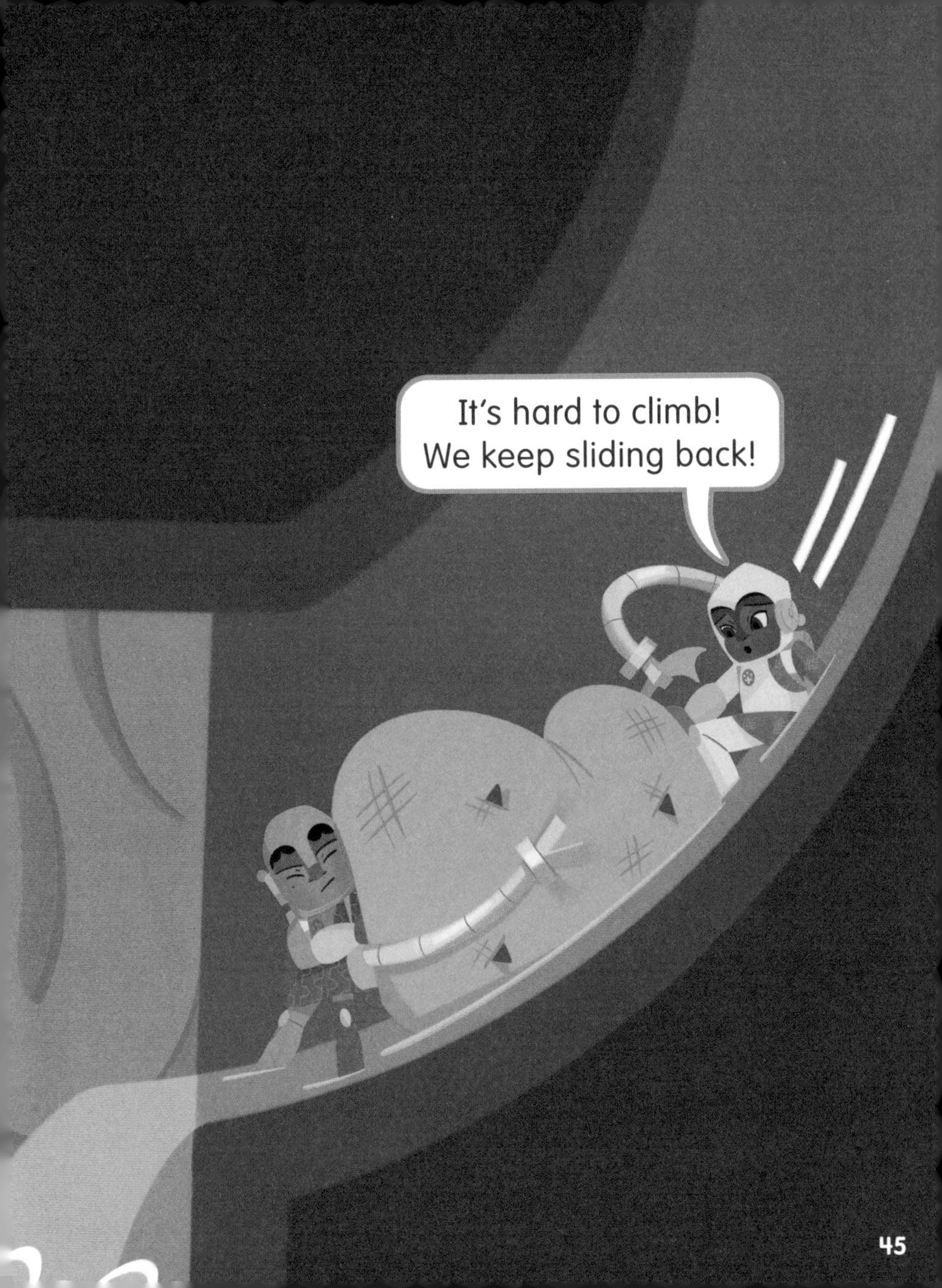
It's hard to climb!
We keep sliding back!

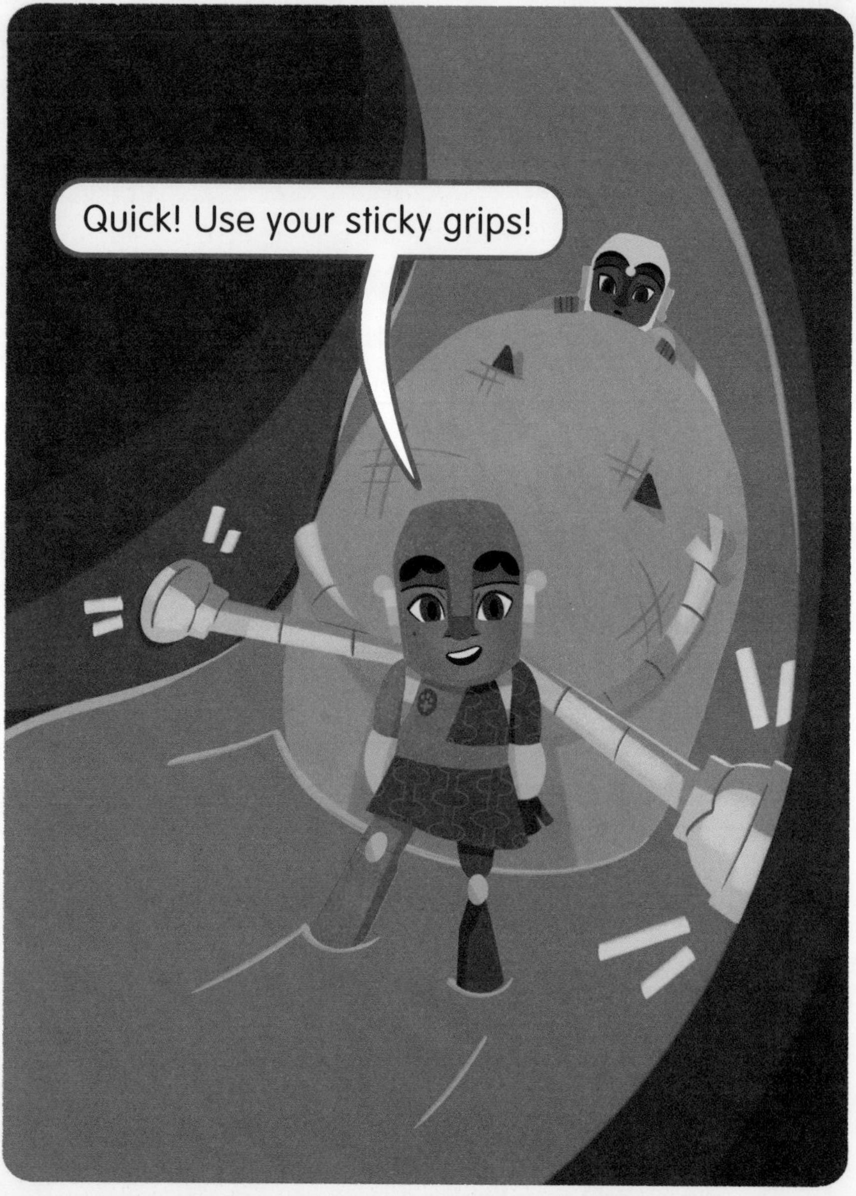
Quick! Use your sticky grips!

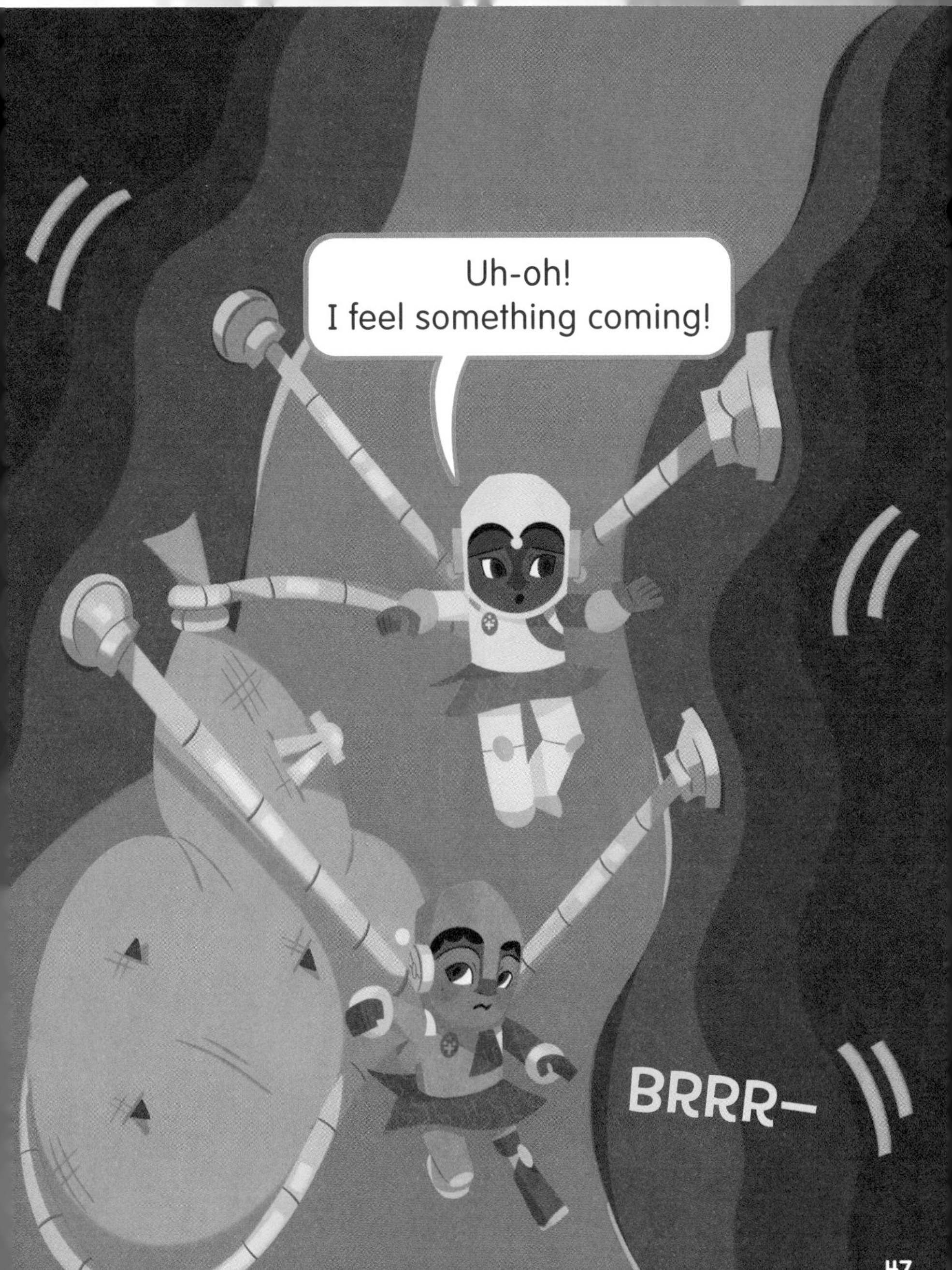
Uh-oh!
I feel something coming!
BRRR–

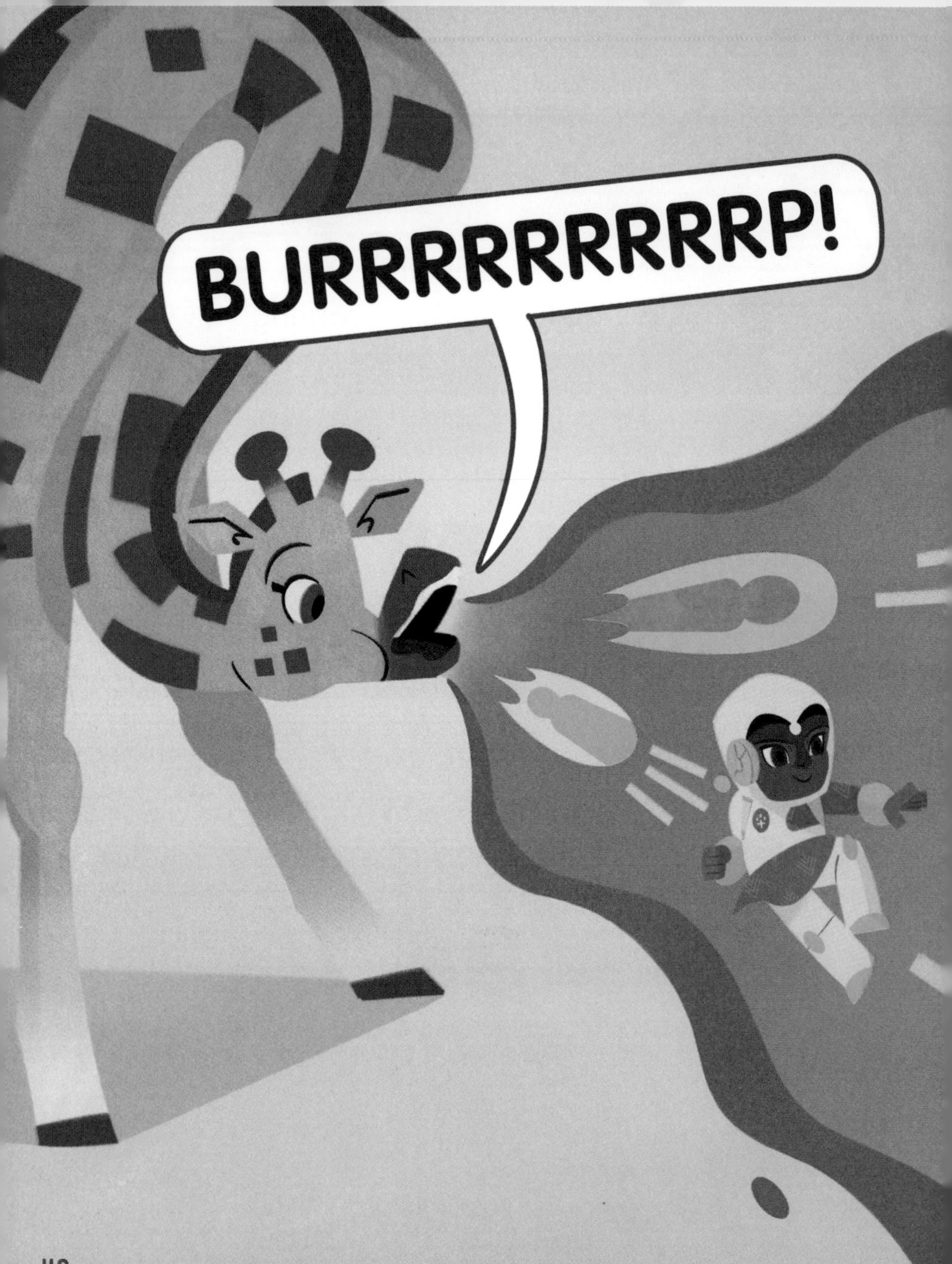
BURRRRRRRRRRP!

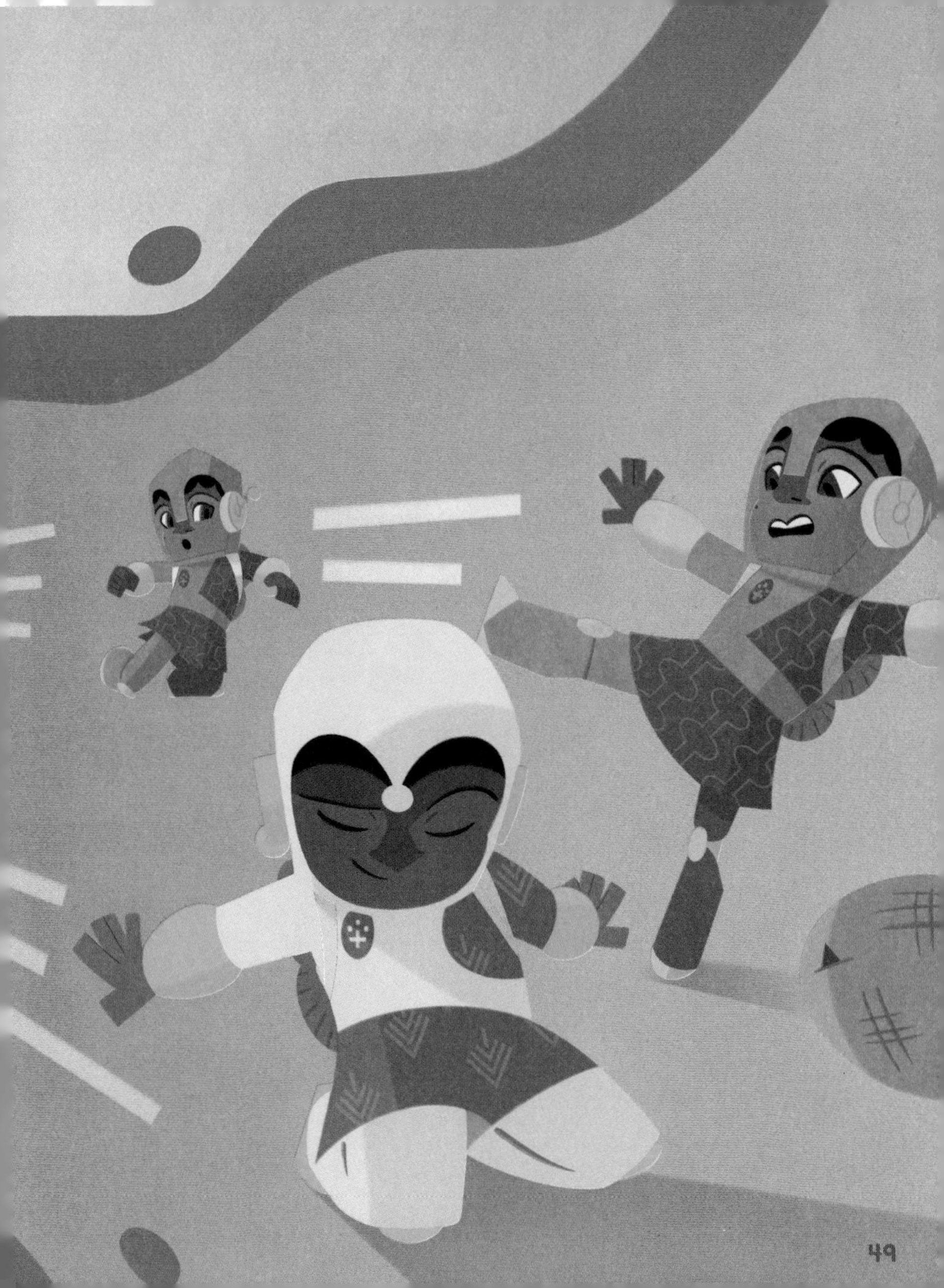

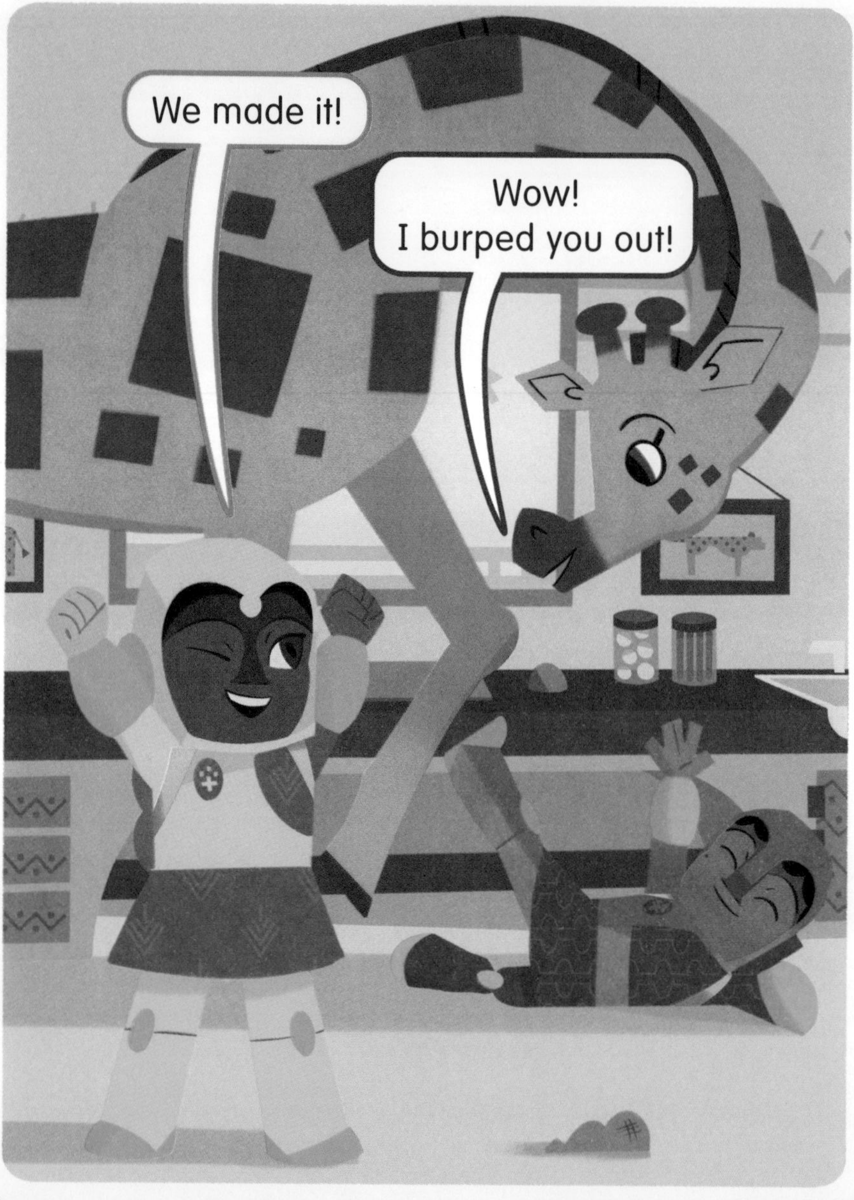
We made it!
Wow!
I burped you out!

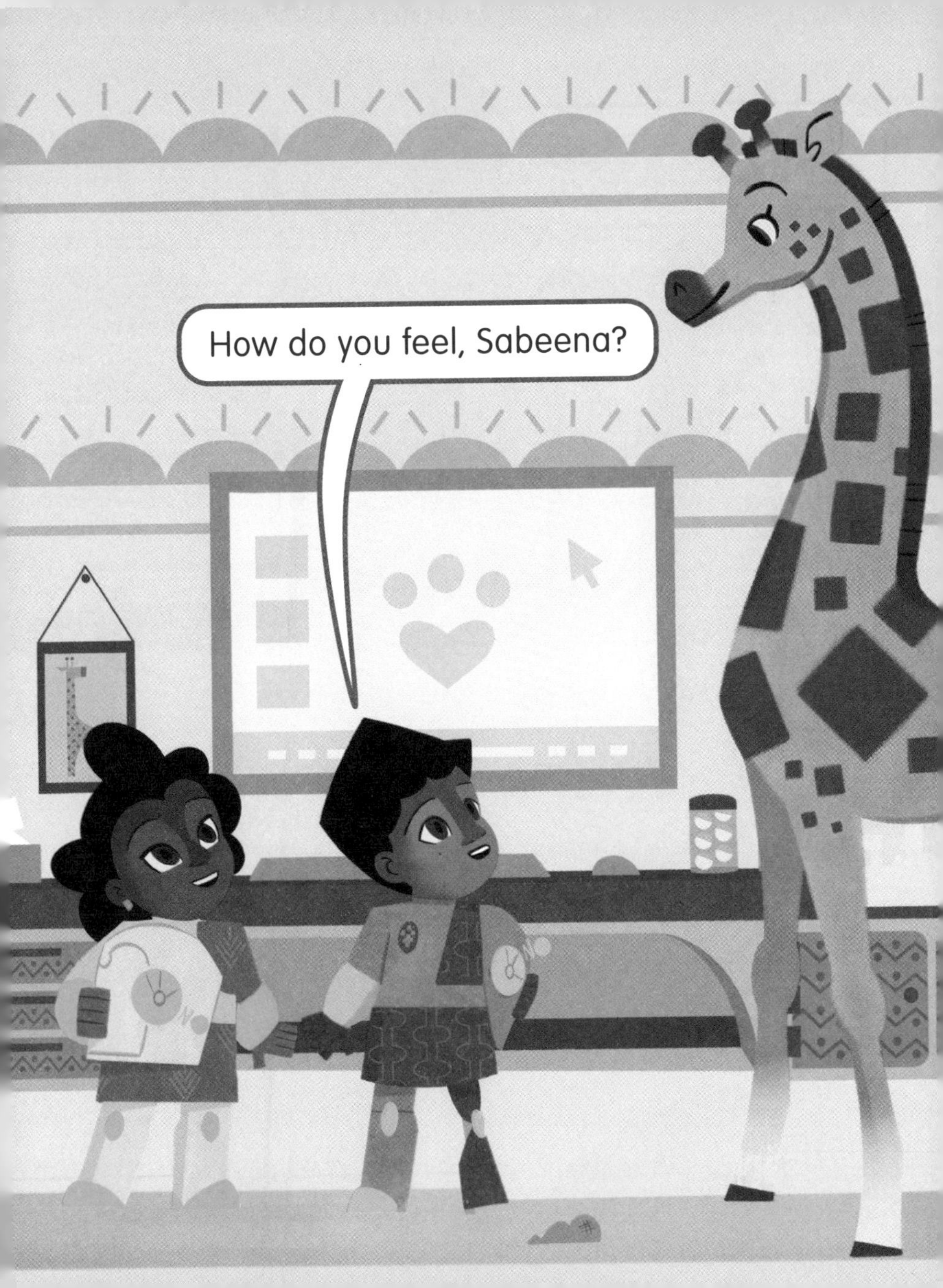
How do you feel, Sabeena?

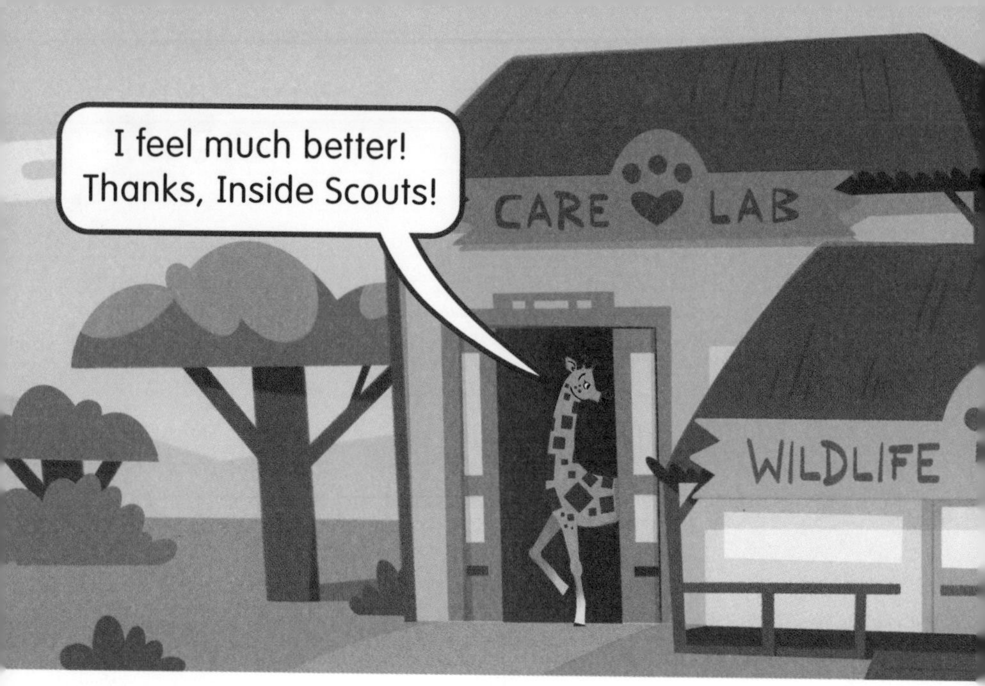
I feel much better!
Thanks, Inside Scouts!
CARE LAB
WILDLIFE

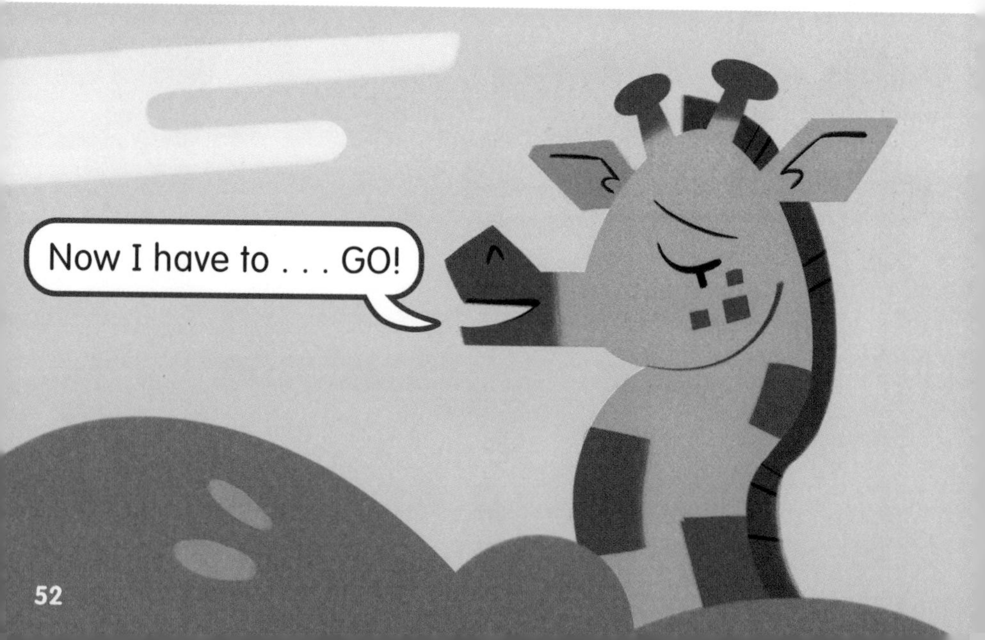
Now I have to . . . GO!

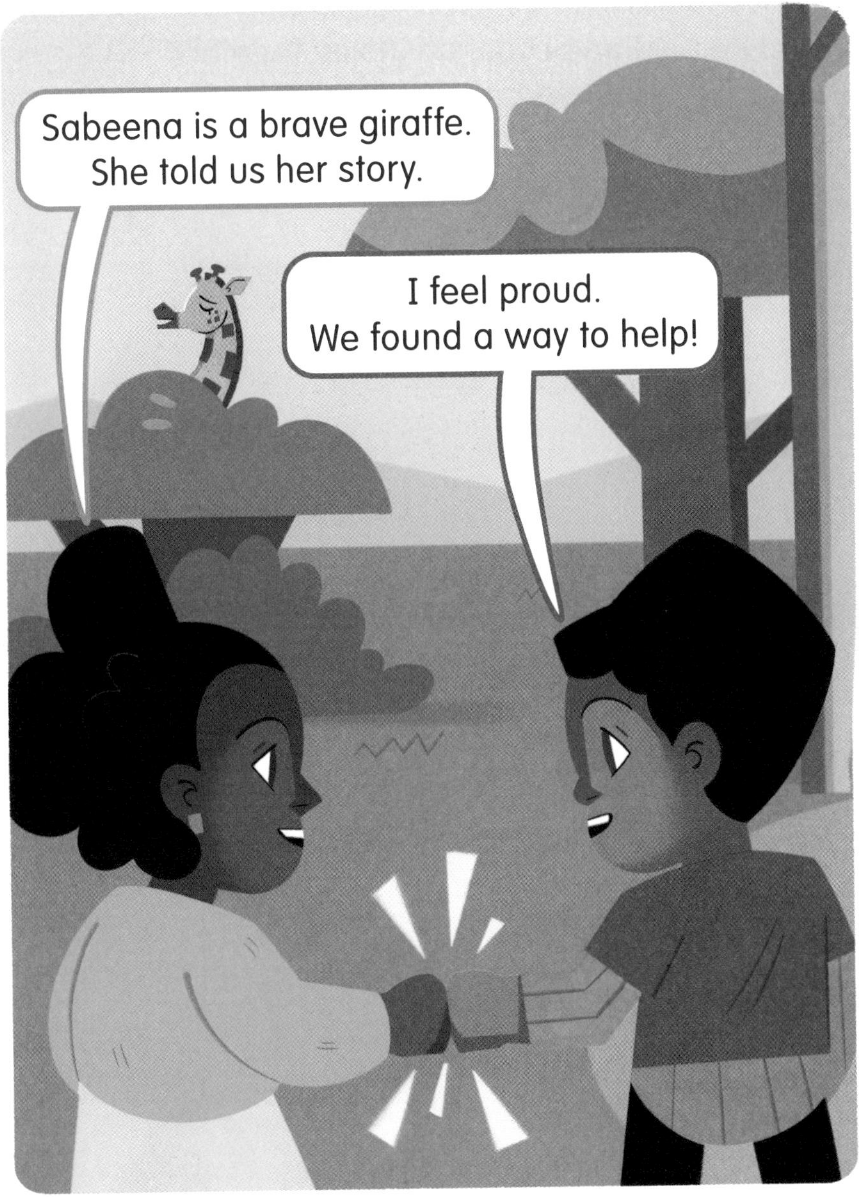
Sabeena is a brave giraffe.
She told us her story.
I feel proud.
We found a way to help!

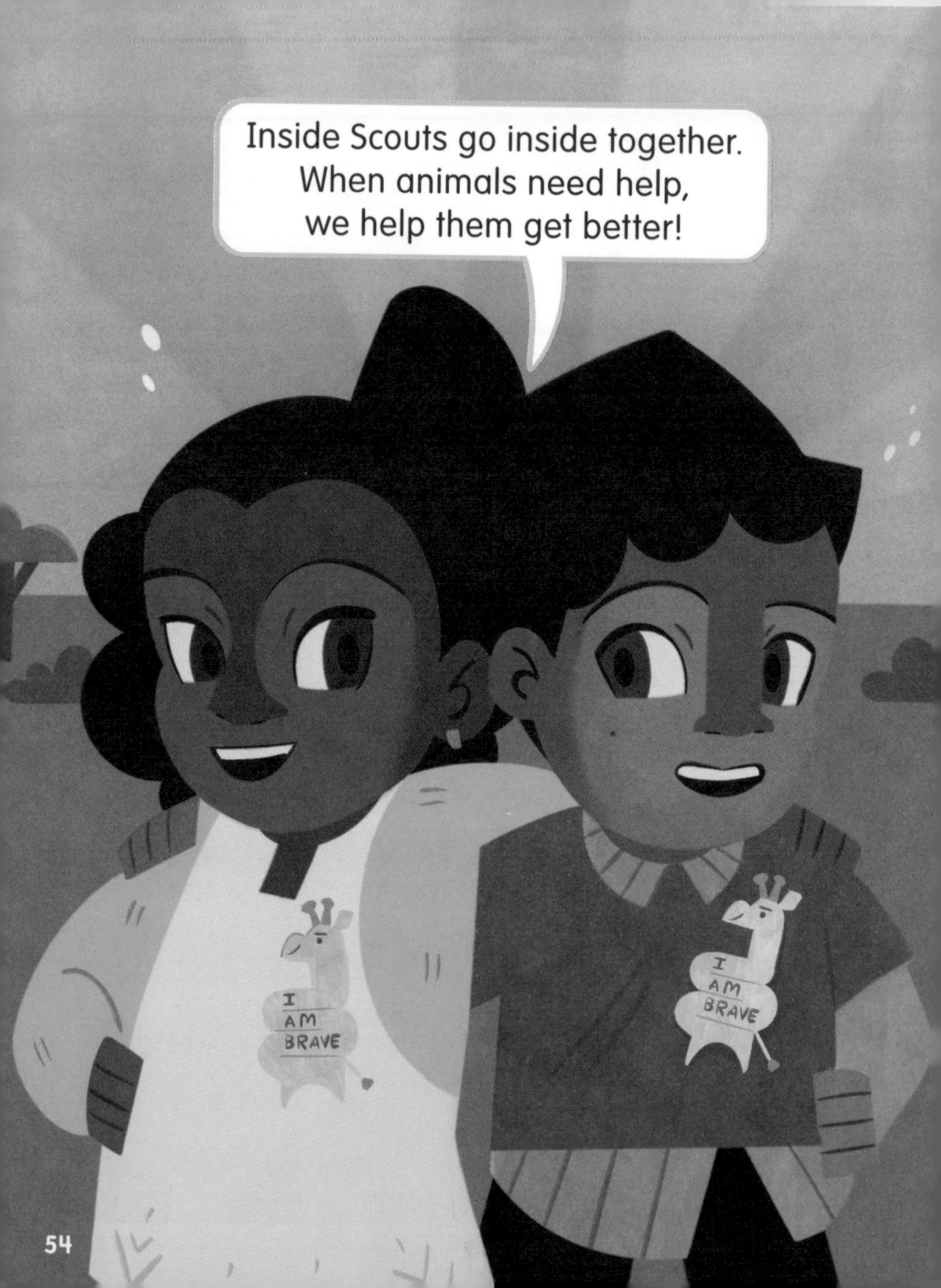
Inside Scouts go inside together. When animals need help, we help them get better!
I AM BRAVE
I AM BRAVE

About the Creators

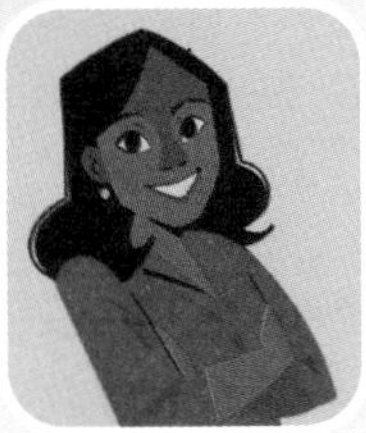

Mitali Banerjee Ruths, MD, was born in New York, grew up in Texas, and now lives in Canada. Before writing books, Mitali studied engineering and medicine.

The idea for The Inside Scouts combines her love for technology, medicine, animals, and the inner workings of our bodies!

The Inside Scouts is Mitali's first early reader series. She is also the author of the early chapter book series The Party Diaries.

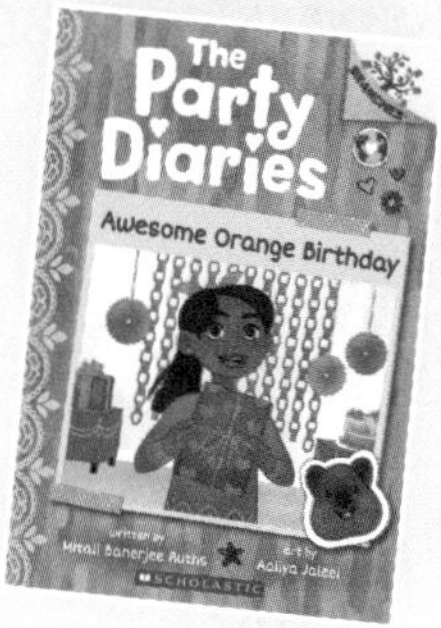
The Party Diaries
Awesome Orange Birthday
Mitali Banerjee Ruths
Aaliya Jaleel
SCHOLASTIC

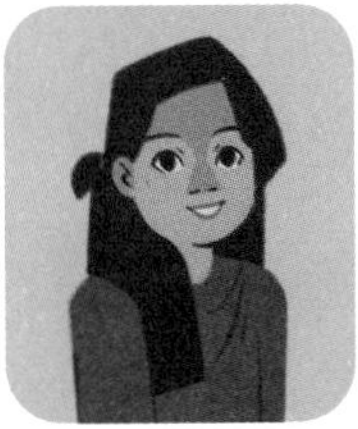

Francesca Mahaney was born and raised in western Massachusetts. She studied illustration in New York City before returning to the quiet woods of New England. Currently, she lives with her three wild cats—Beauregard, Melody, and Sherwin.

The Inside Scouts is Francesca's first early reader series.

Fun Facts about the Gut

1. The gut is part of the **digestive** (dye-JES-tiv) system. The gut is made up of many parts: **mouth**, **esophagus** (i-SAH-fuh-guhs), **stomach** (STUHM-uhk), **small intestine** (in-TES-tin), **colon** (KOH-luhn), and **anus** (AY-nuhs).

2. The parts of the gut connect to make one long, stretchy tube. Food gets squeezed down the tube so our gut can **digest** (dye-JEST) or turn what we eat into building blocks and energy for our bodies.

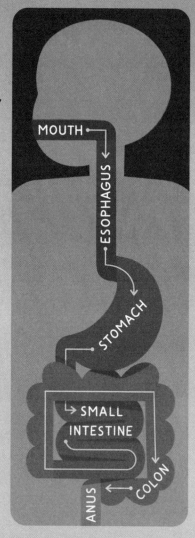

MOUTH

ESOPHAGUS

STOMACH

SMALL INTESTINE

COLON

ANUS

3 The gut turns food into **nutrients** (NOO-tree-uhnts). That's the stuff we need to stay alive! Then the rest of the food turns into poop!

FOOD
NUTRIENTS

4 There is a special gut–brain connection! Our gut can change our mood and energy.

BRAIN
GUT

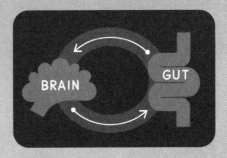

5 The gut is also home to a world of tiny living things! This amazing world inside our gut is called the **microbiome** (mye-kroh-BYE-ohm). It helps us stay healthy.

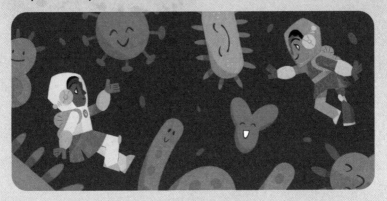

DRAW YOUR OWN "I AM BRAVE" BADGE!

1 Draw five lines that are about these lengths.

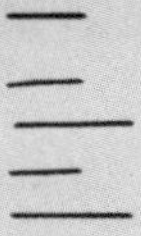

2 Join the lines with four bumps.

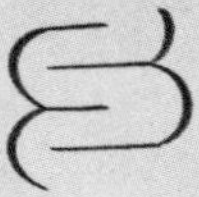

3 Draw four vertical lines, for the outside of the neck and legs.

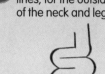

4 Make the head. Draw a swoop to show two legs.

5 Add a face, two horns, one ear, and a tail. Then write "I AM BRAVE."

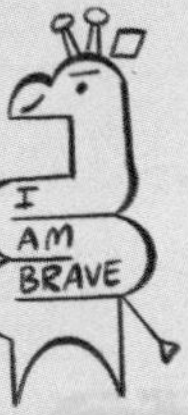

6 Color in your drawing!

WHAT'S YOUR STORY?

Being brave means trying something new or hard, even when we feel scared or worried.
You can be brave with what you say and how you act.
How can **you** be brave by trying something new?
Write and draw your story!
Then go do your brave action!

scholastic.com/acorn